THE SALT IN THE SEA

J. D. RIVERS

DUCK
PRINTS
PRESS

Schenectady, New York

This book is a work of fiction. The characters and events portrayed are a product of the author's imagination. Any resemblance to real people or events is coincidental.

The Salt in the Sea
Copyright © 2025 J. D. Rivers

Front cover design by planetsandmagic

Edited by boneturtle, Nina Waters, and Owl Outerbridge
Print manuscript formatting by Hermit Prints
E-book formatting by Nina Waters

Published by Duck Prints Press, LLC
Schenectady, New York
duckprintspress.com

ISBN (ePub Edition): 978-1-962488-27-3
ISBN (PDF Edition): 978-1-962488-28-0
ISBN (Print edition): 978-1-962488-29-7

Tags:
Genre: Mystery in a Fantasy with Technology Setting
Rating: General Audiences
Trigger Warnings: drowning, speciesism
Relationships: friends with benefits (mentions of), interspecies relationship, m/m
Character Features: gay, half-human, has a disability, magic use, mercenary, murderer, non-human character, orphan, phobia (thalassophobia), ptsd, scars, selkie, veteran, werewolf
Other Tags: attraction at first sight, be gay solve crimes, bittersweet ending, emotional hurt/comfort, false accusations, fraught family dynamics, mating bonds, misunderstandings, murder, one-night stand, past tense, pining (mutual), possessive behavior, second chances, sexual content (non-graphic descriptions), smoking (casual), third person limited (multiple) point of view

CONTENTS

Chapter 1

"Why me?" Victor Lucien watched his companion over the rim of his coffee cup. The coffee was cheap and burned.

Stephen McKinley shrugged. For a man of his size, he shrugged rather delicately, almost with a dancer's grace: forward, up, and down. "You and me? We've seen some shit."

Some military-grade shit—hunting down elder dragons in the desert, wrestling with trolls in mountain caves, dancing with pixies under the starlight, watching rivers flow backward and the moon splinter. He, Stephen, and their team had seen some real shit when they served together.

Victor put his mug down and steepled his fingers together.

Stephen smirked at the gesture, and Victor barely suppressed his own smile. How often had he done that in mission briefings when the brass were about to lie through their teeth?

"And yet you haven't answered. Why me?"

They went way back, having served together for almost ten years. They'd made a good team but had never seen eye to eye. Stephen had a volatile streak that had gotten them into hot waters more than once, and more often than Victor cared for. But they'd parted amicably.

Stephen watched Victor, and Victor stared back. Stephen wasn't a bad-looking guy, all square jaw and military-grade buzz cut, with dark, intense eyes and a soft mouth. "The grapevine says you're strapped for money."

"Me and everyone in this economy." Victor flagged down the waitress and held up his cup so she could refill it. He took a sip and grimaced. It hadn't gotten magically better. The pot had definitely stayed on the warmer for too long. It had almost a syrup-like consistency.

"Come down from your high horse. You've got no job and you're already behind on your rent."

"Do I want to know how you got that information?"

Stephen smiled sharply and spread his fingers in a *what do you think?* gesture. He hadn't even touched his coffee.

Victor had tried to find a job, but with his heritage, it had been...difficult. Being a half-werewolf was apparently good enough for fighting, but not for civilian life.

Some cross-breeds were lucky and didn't carry signs of their wolf ancestry into their human form, but on Victor, everything was a bit too much. His ears were too pointy, his hair too shaggy, and his features too sharp. But the worst was the superior sense of smell. The diner smelled of old oil and mold, and Stephen smelled of stale cigarettes and sex. Only Stephen would stumble to a meeting at predawn after a quick tumble, and only Stephen would be eyeing the waitress with equal amounts disgust and lust. Stephen hated everything that he didn't perceive as normal. But normal was, for him, a pretty adaptable standard.

Victor had tried to be a private security officer, a cashier, and a dock worker, hoping that manual labor at least was open to him. But his bluntness had landed him in trouble with the customers and his colleagues. His superior sense of smell had creeped out almost everyone, and his temper had flared every time he'd been faced with stupidity and incompetence. He'd always thought the brass were the pinnacle of imbecility, but entitled customers made an art form out of it.

"So, you are doing this from the bottom of your heart? Spare me," Victor answered.

Stephen smiled in kind, showing off the rows of his sharp teeth. "I know you can handle it. And the fact that you can actually use the money doesn't hurt." Stephen tapped his fingers on the table. "You can take it or leave it." He took out his wallet and handed over a card. "Call me when you've decided. But don't take too long, I don't run a charity." He put the card between them and added some crumpled notes, enough to cover the coffee and an entire meal, the little shit. He stopped at Victor's side and squeezed his shoulder.

"Nice seeing you again, Vic." He left with a lopsided smile and a smell that made Victor sick. It spoke of pure sexual desire with a heavy undertone of revulsion. Victor wondered why it had never bothered him when Stephen and he had used each for mutual release.

The waitress materialized beside him. Victor believed her to be at least part pixie, with enough power to read superfluous desires but not enough to join her sisters out in the ancient woods and weave dreams. She smiled at him, her pad at the ready. "That will be the breakfast platter?"

He only nodded, and with another smile, she was gone.

Victor picked up the card.

Stephen McKinley
Security Consultant
35076183515

All very cloak-and-dagger. "Security Consultant" was an odd designation for a mercenary who ran underground, which was the last profession Victor had heard about him doing. Stephen had left the military shortly after Victor. Rumor was, the brass had encouraged him to leave so he wouldn't get a dishonorable discharge. Victor had pressed to learn more, but all parties involved had been close-mouthed.

He needed to go by the facts. On the surface, the job was simple: ship over to a remote island, get a package handed to him, come back, and collect the money. But nothing with Stephen had ever been easy. No one sent an ex-special-ops officer to receive some pesky package, regardless of how much of an old buddy he was or how much he needed the money. Stephen expected resistance. And it was Victor's job to take care of that resistance.

As the waitress came fluttering back, he put the card into his breast pocket and moved his cup to the side to make room for the eggs, sausages, and toast. He gave the waitress a smile, which she took with a flush and hurried away. Whether from embarrassment or fear, he couldn't tell.

While he shoveled in the food, he looked up the island Stephen wanted him to go to on his phone. It was small, just off-coast, close yet remote. It had a small town and was inhabited by various magical folk. On the far side was a small werewolf settlement. Victor paused. Werewolves were territorial, wary of outsiders coming too close to what they considered theirs. At the slightest hint of something off, they closed ranks. Only other werewolves had a chance of an in. Well, that would explain Stephen's interest in getting Victor on the job.

Having polished everything off the plates, he rose and

added a few coins as a tip to the crumpled bills. Stephen had been stingy. He nodded at the waitress and the cook, who'd been watching him with narrowed eyes, and stepped out.

Victor knew he would call Stephen. They both knew it. It was good and fast money, and he really needed it. People feared him, even without knowing that he was part werewolf. They only took a glance at him, broad-shouldered, big, scarred, with shaggy hair, and then he was out again. They changed to the other side of the sidewalk, even in the light of day. It didn't matter that he'd served the country, that he was a veteran and just trying to live. They only saw their own fear.

Victor walked the few blocks to his shabby apartment. The old lady on the first floor peered at him through the dirty window, frowning—she always frowned. The family on the second floor was having a row again, their small son sitting out in the hall playing with beat-up toy cars. Victor sneaked him one of the hard candies he'd taken to carrying around since he had moved in here a few years ago. The boy smiled at him and went back to playing. Kids only feared when their parents told them to fear. The smell of pot lingered in the air when he crossed the hall by apartment number four, occupied by a small man who always snickered. Victor put him down as being a leprechaun. They were quite rare and harmless, but never stopped laughing.

Victor let himself into his apartment on the fifth, and last, floor. The only redeeming qualities were the view and easy access to the roof where he could catch some fresh air when the walls closed in again. Maybe after the job, it would be time to move. He'd held onto the city long enough waiting for...something. Three years he'd waited while life moved around him. Victor had shoved the feelings of being stuck to the side and concentrated on something that had been almost within his reach, but it—he—had never returned. It was high time Victor let go.

The military had given him purpose. He'd been good at his job. Tracking down the monsters and taking them out had been easy. As an orphaned were with a not-so-stellar school record—he'd barely graduated—going into service for the pay had been a no-brainer. The higher-ups had soon discovered his superior tracking and fighting skills—and his utter lack of remorse. And, while he hadn't been accepted there, either, he'd had at least the respect of his team. They'd trusted him enough to cover their backs, and to let him lead.

Victor tapped the card against a rickety sideboard in the hallway, thinking.

They said the south was friendlier to mixed races. It was also warmer and sunnier, not rain- and wind-encrusted like here. He took the card and was already typing on the phone with his other hand before he realized he was doing it.

It rang three times.

"So, come to your senses?" The voice was smug through the speaker.

"Just tell me when and where."

A leap, and the boat dropped down again. Victor nearly tore a piece out of the railing while gripping it. The old captain cackled in his cabin. His eyes were focused on the rough sea. His weathered face, and the wisp of white hair that peeked out from under his woolen cap, gave the impression of an old sea bear. Victor whiffed some magic around him, but it was too faint and too watered down to pinpoint. Probably some sea creature very far down the family line.

Not that it mattered. Victor eyed the dark, rolling water around them with trepidation. He hadn't many fears; they'd been blown away between the desert heat and the clashing of mountains. When darkness had looked back at him with yellow, blinking eyes and hollow laughter, he'd learned to roll with it. But water...he shook his head.

Off-white blinked through the stormy sea, dark eyes watching him lazily before they disappeared again.

Victor swallowed, his eyes searching for the captain.

"You saw the monster?" the captain shouted over the thundering water.

"The monster?"

"Aye, they say a kraken lives down here, waiting to hunt, waiting to take, waiting for the right prey." Another of those cackles.

Victor gulped but let it go. On unsteady legs, he walked to the cabin and clawed his hands into the frame. He had stepped outside to get his rolling nausea under control; it had now been washed away by pure fear.

Should they make it to the harbor, he'd call Stephen and ask for more money. When they'd set out from the mainland, the weather had been all right. No wind, no clouds in the sky. But the captain had barely looked at him, started the engine, and told him to hold on tight. Half the way over, the sky had darkened and the wind had picked up.

"The island doesn't like visitors. Every time I ship over, it tries to dispel me, but in this battle of wills, I win." He had screamed the last bit into the wind, and a particularly vicious wave, thundering against the boat's side, had been the answer. The captain had grinned and shipped on.

Insane.

And Victor was even crazier for stepping onto this ship. He braced himself as another high wave came in.

This would be what finally did him in.

And then, just like that, the sea stretched calmly before them under a startling blue sky. Above them, a seagull cried. Victor blinked into the sun. "Am I dead?"

"No, youngster. We made it." And then he sang. His voice rang loud and clear over the water. Victor didn't know the language—it sounded guttural and ancient. The water slapped gently against the boat's side, as if it was clapping in rhythm. Maybe this was the captain's payment, his offering to the ancient magic that ruled the waters and the island.

It took them half an hour longer, but then they were moored against the landing. Three men waited already. They all had their arms crossed, but their faces were relaxed. They laughed at something one of them said. No one else waited with them.

"Are there any waiting travelers?" asked Victor.

"They never leave the island," the captain said. "They are born here, and they die here. What they need, I bring over. There are seldom visitors." The captain eyed him as he said that but didn't ask, though his eyes lingered on Victor's face and ears. Victor knew what he must be thinking: one more to join the fray.

Victor shouldered his pack when the ship was secured. "When will you be back?"

"To take you over again?" The captain mussed with his beard as he nodded at the men who started hauling out the goods. They all three threw Victor a curious glance, but none stopped to inquire about him. "I won't be back for at least a week. The weather will rough up, and it'll be too dangerous to ship over." He blinked. "You've a place to stay?"

"I'll try the local inn." The island had one; Victor had checked before he left. He'd tried to contact them to reserve a place, but there had been no number nor email listed.

The captain leaned against the railing, his gaze sweeping over the small town, then he smiled. "They've one. I'm also sure they've rooms. But the owner is a bit peculiar."

Victor shrugged. He hoped for a roof over his head, but he could also camp outside. He'd packed for the eventuality automatically. A lightweight sleeping bag. A small tent, easily assembled and disassembled. Even after four years out, packing the military way was ingrained into him.

"Thanks," he said, and held out his hand, massive and almost claw-like. The captain didn't bat an eye and shook it. Then, he shouted for the unloaders, and Victor knew he'd been dismissed.

When Victor set foot onto the shore, the world shifted sideways for a second before he was accustomed to solid ground again. Victor blinked into the blue sky and exhaled. No one came running, demanding to know what he was doing here and forcing him off the island.

So far, so good.

He fished his phone out from a side-pocket on his pack and checked the connectivity. Two bars. Not bad. He'd downloaded the island map before setting sail to be on the safe side, but maybe the modern world had reached even this remote place. He called up the address of the inn and found it was roughly a twenty-minute walk, situated just outside of the small village on the eastern side of the island, close to the water.

Even if the owner of the inn wouldn't offer him a bed, he'd deal with it as he dealt with everything in his life: work with or around it.

The village was nice enough. Most houses were clustered, as far as Victor could see, around a central plaza with an obelisk in the middle. The obelisk was black and somber, almost like the one his unit had seen atop a witch tower. That one had radiated pure maliciousness. This one didn't seem to have any magic, and yet Victor caught the impression of a warning: the island was watching.

Victor walked up the small road. An old woman stared at him, then hurried along. Victor ignored her. The air was fresh and breezy, and green pastures opened up when he stepped out from the rows of residential buildings. Farther in the distance, he could make out the inn wedged between two cliffs. It was a low two-story building, and behind it the gray sea rolled to the horizon.

Gravel crunched under his boots when the cobblestone changed to dirt road. The sun was high in the sky, and sweat trickled down his back. A lone seagull squawked, and the sound mixed with the faint tinkle of sheep bells in the distance.

This felt like actual peace.

Maybe he should treat his time here as some kind of vacation. For one week, he didn't need to worry about food or rent or where he would get the money to pay for either. For one week, he could lie back and just be. Even if he had no clue how.

The road came at an angle to the inn. To the side, Victor spotted cliffs and the shimmer of a pebbled beach. The house sat smack in the middle of the cliff opening. Victor wondered if someone had specifically made the opening to build the inn or if it had formed naturally. Either way, the building fit perfectly. The peak of the blue roof was almost level with the rocky tops, and between the side-walls and the gray stone, there was barely an inch. One could probably wander from one side of the cliff to the other and use the roof as a bridge.

The house itself was formed from the same light stone as the buildings down in the village, with matching blue window frames and a blue door. Flowers had uncurled in small beds to either side of the door. A lazy bumblebee circled Victor once, twice, before buzzing away.

Was all this really needed to get a package from A to B? Stephen had stressed the fragility of the cargo, but what could be so fragile that he'd entrusted Victor with it personally, and even would pay him to stay on this island?

Or was it that the wolves had their hands in it, and that Stephen needed another wolf to cut through the posturing and conduct business? They could be awfully closed off if crossed.

Victor sighed, then used the old-fashioned knocker at the door.

For a long moment, nothing happened. Victor checked his phone and, to his dismay, all the bars had gone and the signal was dead. But he was at the right door. This was the inn.

He knocked again. Something fell over inside, there was a curse, and then the door wrenched open.

"What?"

Victor paused. "You?"

CHAPTER 2

"ME?" ICE-BLUE eyes blinked up at Victor.

Victor reconsidered. Recognition had flooded all his senses, but now...there was something off about this person. He was similar in build and stature to the memory swirling through Victor's mind. Smaller than Victor, with dirty blond hair and those sky-blue eyes. Even his magic was similar, but somehow burned-off at the edges, just shy of being repulsive.

He didn't show a hint of recognition.

Victor swallowed. "I apologize." He paused, the sense of familiarity not dissipating. "Are you sure we haven't met before?"

The other narrowed his eyes. "If that's all?" he asked, and started closing the door.

Victor shot out his hand and pressed the door back.

That carned him an irritated scowl. "What now?"

"I'd like to book a room."

"You want to book a room?"

"This is the inn, isn't it?" Victor craned his neck to check the plaque at the side of the door. "Stormbeach Inn" was embossed in big bold letters. A bit dramatic, in Victor's opinion, but undeniable.

"This is the inn," the other repeated cautiously, as if he wasn't sure what Victor was getting at. Was it so surprising that someone would come and actually ask for a room? Otherwise, why would there be an inn here?

"Look, the ferry won't be back for a week, and I'll need a room until then."

"What are you doing here?"

"Business in the village," Victor said, shifting the pack on his back.

"What business could there possibly be in the village?"

Victor smiled, the kind that wouldn't reach his eyes. "That is none of your business." He gestured at the house. "So you got a room or not? If not, I will camp somewhere, if you'd at least be so kind as to point to a place where I'm allowed to?"

The scowl deepened. "There's a storm coming. Outdoor camping is not advised."

"So, what will it be then?"

"Keep your knickers on. If it can't be avoided, I have a room for you." He stepped back, keeping his eyes on Victor a second longer before he turned and walked away.

Victor took that as the only invitation he'd get and stepped in. The hallway was dark and musty. On a small table to the side was a thick layer of dust. To his left, stairs led up into an even gloomier darkness. The innkeeper had stepped into a small room to the right, and Victor followed into what seemed to be the reception area, with a dark wooden counter and even more dust. It tickled his nose and throat, but he didn't give in to the sneeze.

The innkeeper opened a drawer and fished out two keys, then stepped around Victor and to the stairs. He pointed down the hallway leading away from the entry door. "The second room to the right is the dining room. I will put out breakfast there. Don't expect anything fancy. Dinner will be in the pub in the village; I will inform the owner." Then he pointed to the left. "Behind the stairs is the entry to the living room, which also holds the library. You're free to borrow and read any book. I'll be out most of the day; I have a bookstore at the village square." He went up, and Victor followed dutifully. At the top, he held up the keys. "Water view or inland?"

"Water view." Victor was not a friend of water or the sea, and yet whenever he was close to it, the soft sloshing of the waves was soothing. Had always been soothing, even—

The innkeeper handed him a room key, the number embossed on it, and pointed to the door with the same number. "The key also works on the front door. I'll leave the check-in form on the dining room table. The bed is made, the towels are on the table, and the bath is down the hall." He pointed to the left, down a row of maybe five more rooms. "But every room has a sink. The attic is off limits." He crossed his arms. "Anything else?"

"Your name?" He couldn't keep calling him "the innkeeper."

"Thoma." Then he turned and walked down the stairs. Victor followed the sound of his steps through the house until a door opened and closed, and then only silence remained. For a second, Victor wondered where his life had gone wrong, but then he shook himself out of it and opened his room.

Thoma cursed and mumbled all the way from the inn to the pub. He'd only been at the inn because Old Man Nathaniel had wanted to stop by and check on him. He was sure that if he hadn't been there, they wouldn't have a guest.

A guest.

Wasn't that mind boggling? They never had guests. At least none that didn't have relations to someone on the island. And that someone would either have put the person up themselves, or at least tell him to expect someone.

And it was *him*. Of all the inns in this country... Oh, he had recognized the man. How could Thoma ever forget those broad shoulders and that fierce gaze? That night so long ago had been the one time he'd given in and allowed himself to be something more, something different. Just one night before— He swallowed the bile down.

It didn't matter anymore.

Thoma could handle a guest for a week, probably. He sighed. His family was due to gather in a few days, everyone coming to this island, and Old Man Nathaniel had tasked him with the preparations. Thoma pinched the bridge of his nose. Why had that man come now? He shook his head and stepped into the pub. A group of old people were playing cards in one corner. The lunch crowd, if he could call them that, had already left, and only the retired remained. Clair, the waitress and daughter of the owner Per, waved him over.

"Don't you look gloomy today."

Thoma scowled.

"He always looks gloomy," one of the elders shouted.

Thoma rolled his eyes while the others cackled.

"What can I get you?"

"Nothing. But tell your dad we have a guest at the inn, so there needs to be dinner."

She stared at him for a second, then laughed. "Good joke."

Thoma leaned his elbows on the counter and hung his

head. "No joke." He looked up and sighed. "A legit guest at the inn. Here for 'business.'" He suppressed the urge to do air quotes. It could be legitimate; stranger things had happened.

The wolves lived on the western side, almost at the opposite shore. They'd never fully integrated into the community. Thoma had no clue what they did, but he knew the guest was a wolf as well—he'd known the first time they met.

"It's a wolf."

Clair squinted at him. "You think they're up to something."

Thoma shrugged.

"Maybe someone here to join them," Clair mused, her eyes darting in the general direction of the wolf community.

Thoma hadn't considered that. But his guest had said he was only staying for a week.

Did his reason for coming here really matter?

"Just feed him." He knocked on the counter and turned to walk out.

"All right. I'll let Pa know."

Thoma nodded and returned to the street, then took a left, walking swiftly, until he was in front of the bookstore. His bookstore. As always, no one was waiting.

The properties had been in the possession of the family for generations. The land they were built on was family land. Neither turned any profit. The bookshop was little more than a glorified library. People traded books in, and the ferry sometimes shipped boxes of new books over. It suited him well enough. It allowed him to read the whole time, far away from the old man's all-too-knowing eyes, demanding that he do something worthwhile with his life like his cousins. His perfect cousins.

The smell of ink and paper, musty and dry, calmed his nerves. It always struck him with awe, the knowledge of long-lost decades, the worlds discovered and explored, the scientific research to be argued against, lives to be lived—everything at his fingertips. Once, while young and foolish, he'd dreamed of going away, and one day, he'd followed that call into the unforgiving world beyond the gray sea. Then he'd lost it all and had come crawling back. Old Man Nathaniel had been gracious about Thoma's foolishness. He'd handed over the keys to the inn and the bookstore and told him to take care of both.

That moment, Thoma had laid his dreams to rest. His life was comfortable, even with his limitations.

But now they had a guest.

He should stop calling him that, and in that tone, as if he was something disdainful, something bad. He wasn't, but he stood for things Thoma had long put behind him. At least, he'd believed he had—no, he had.

Thoma looked around the store in an attempt to distract himself from further thoughts about the man. Nothing was out of place or needed to be cleaned. Thoma sighed and settled behind the counter. He'd just found the right page again, because unlike a sane person, he always forgot to mark the page, when the bell over the door chimed.

Thoma raised his eyes and closed the book again. Trevor was the right-hand of Maxim, the chief of the wolf settlement. For a wolf of Trevor's position, he was on the smaller side compared to Maxim's larger-than-life impression and to the wolf at the inn, but he was no less dangerous. Maybe even more so, because Trevor had fought for his position with tooth and claw. Thoma wondered if Trevor ever smiled.

"Rumor has it you let a guest stay on the island," Trevor said in lieu of a greeting.

"It's an inn." Thoma did his best to not let his annoyance show.

"You could've told him you're booked." Trevor had moved to the counter, leaning casually against it. Trevor didn't do anything casual—ever.

Thoma rolled his eyes. "As if anyone would believe that."

"Tell him he isn't welcome."

"Tell him yourself. He is your kind." Thoma flashed him a smile.

Trevor showed rows of sharp teeth. "Listen, little fish. Don't try my patience." He sniffed the air. "No, he isn't one of us." He spat, then he whirled around and stomped away. The bell protested when Trevor wrenched the door open and banged it closed.

Thoma shook his head. This was precisely the reason he didn't care for wolves. They had dreadful tempers.

Little fish.

He swallowed the flash of pain down and looked back at the book. Traced the words on the cover with his fingers. A promise of adventures and exotic worlds. All the things he would never see.

His stomach churned. He must be hungry, because nothing else was the matter with him, nothing at all.

Just as the sun was setting, Victor stepped out of the inn. Pink and purple were painted in bold stripes across the sky. With the encroaching darkness, the temperature had dropped and the wind had picked up. But it was still pleasant enough for a walk.

Victor checked the post office first. It was dark and shuttered up, the opening times proclaiming it would stay like that for the next two days. Marvelous. Victor sighed and returned to the main street. He sidestepped an older lady who watched him with hooded eyes. Was she the same one as before? There weren't many people on the streets. The total population of the village wasn't more than a couple hundred souls—at least that was what the information he could find indicated. The island was otherwise shrouded in mystery, or at least not important enough for a detailed account to have been taken of the day-to-day lives of its inhabitants.

The world saw strange things on a daily basis; a remote island no one seemed to have heard of wasn't the most unique thing.

Unsure what to do next, he turned toward the harbor...and his stomach growled.

The pub was easy to find. It was the only brightly lit building, a few blocks down. Music and laughter spilled out of the windows, thrown open to let the breeze through the barroom.

And yet, as soon as he set his foot inside, the laughter ceased. Only the music, a sorrowful old shanty, soldiered on.

A small woman with reddish-brown hair and freckles materialized next to him. With a professional smile, she pointed him to a corner table. He nodded gratefully and walked over. He resisted making eye contact with anyone and settled with his back to the wall. Slowly, the other guests' eyes slid away, and the conversations started again.

The woman returned to him. "I'm Clair. My father runs the pub," she said cheerily. "Dinner is steak and chips. What can I get you to drink?"

"A cider," Victor said after glancing at the chalkboard over the bar.

"Aye, steak medium?"

He nodded, and with another smile, Clair flitted away. She smelled of sunshine and rainbows but was missing the more dark magic associated with the fae folk. Victor wondered briefly if she had resisted the call of the other-side-court, or if she had never been summoned.

A few minutes later, Clair put a glass with cider to his right and hurried away again as someone called for her.

Victor kept his head down. The murmurs ebbed and flowed around him: shouts to new arrivals, calls for Clair or the pub owner, comments on the weather or the migration of the fish and the monster of the deep. Ordinary conversations, and yet the easy laughter from before was gone. From time to time, he felt their eyes on him, the big, burly werewolf sulking in the corner trespassing on another tribe's territory.

Victor counted the minutes, waiting for something.

In the end, it happened at the same time his food arrived. When Clair put the dish in front of him—it smelled heavenly, rich and earthy—the room fell quiet. Victor cut into the meat, speared the piece with his fork, and took a bite. He chewed slowly while heavy boots thumped closer. A chair was dragged out, then a massive body fell into it. The chair groaned, and Victor swallowed his food down.

He flicked his gaze up while he cut the next piece, taking in the scene. Six pairs of amber glowing eyes. Three wolves. Their heavy, funky scent tickled Victor's nostrils. One had a blond buzzcut and a deep scowl. He stood to the left, just beyond the shoulder of the sitting wolf. Second-in-command, then. The wolf to the other side had his arms crossed. He looked older than the left one, studying

Victor, projecting calm. That made the one in the middle the leader. His hair was long and silvery, his face riddled with lines, one prominent scar over his left eye.

Victor took the next bite and chewed.

That got him a snarl from the second-in-command.

A hothead for a second-in-command, a bold choice.

"Be quiet, Trevor." The leader's voice was deep and calm.

"But—"

"It would be a waste to let good food go cold," said the leader. Trevor crossed his arms and turned his head away. "Go get me an ale." The moment stretched on, then Trevor retreated. The ambient noise picked up once more. "I apologize for him."

Victor shrugged, took another bite, chewed, and swallowed. "He's young."

"He should still know better."

They sat in silence while Victor chased the last bit of sauce with the last chip. The second guard didn't even twitch. Victor moved the empty dish away and picked up his glass. Only then did he allow himself to take a better look. The leader of the wolves was older than Victor had initially thought. One could see it in his eyes and in the folds around his neck. But he still radiated power and authority.

Trevor came back, put the ale down at the chief's elbow, and—after a pointed look from the leader—slunk to a nearby table, trying to appear as if he wasn't listening in.

"I'm Maxim, and this is Sea Gull Island." He made a sweeping gesture.

Victor extended his hand. "I'm Victor."

Maxim nodded and shook his hand. Then he took a sip of his ale, his eyes never leaving Victor's. "What brings you to this place, Victor?"

"Business."

"There isn't much business one could conduct here. And we know those who come and go to conduct said business." Maxim took another sip. "We do not know you."

Victor took a sip of his own drink. He loved the mix of alcohol and the ripe sweetness of apples. It had been one of the things he'd missed when he had been deployed in the desert. "I'll be gone in a week when the ferry returns."

"Is that so?"

Victor shrugged in a take-it-or-leave-it gesture.

Maxim nodded as if Victor was telling him something he was already aware of. He'd probably asked the captain, maybe someone else. It didn't matter. Victor would be gone in a week, and he wouldn't challenge Maxim for his position or interfere in any matter of the tribe. That was all Maxim was interested in.

"One week." With those parting words Maxim rose, knocked on the wood, and sauntered to a table on the other side, followed by his henchman. Victor watched him greet the people at the table, then Victor drained his glass and waved Clair over.

"I'd like to pay."

Clair shook her head. "Everything you eat and drink will be put on the tab. Thoma will get a bill every morning. You'll pay at the end of your stay."

Victor nodded and thanked her for the food. When he crossed the barroom, the noise fell away again, and Victor hoped that this wouldn't happen every time he twitched a toe.

He stepped out into the night. The breeze had picked up even more. The sky was clear, and stars dotted the darkness stretching above. He hadn't seen the stars in a long time. In the desert, it had been almost overwhelming, the band of the Milky Way stretching like a glittering ribbon, dwarfing one's existence into something tiny and foolish. In the city, only the strongest and brightest stars could be seen through the pollution that had gotten worse while he'd been away.

Here, it was dark enough that he would be able to sleep without having to shut any blinking neon lights out. And yet a slight glow remained, enough that there wasn't a danger of falling into the sky when he looked at it too long. He crammed his hands into his pockets. There wasn't a soul on the street with him. He breathed in the crisp air and tasted a salty tang. The desert air had been dry and smelled slightly burned. The city was overwhelming and nauseating. Maybe he could explore while he waited to get his hands on the package. Stretching his legs on long walks sounded like heaven.

The inn was dark. Victor let himself in. There was no sound, no movement. The house had the quality of emptiness. He moved through the shadows and up the stairs with careful, deliberate steps, waiting for the ambush, waiting for the darkness to move and reach for him. Wolves could only see contrast better in the darkness, they didn't have the fabled night vision people thought they had. Sudden lights blinded them. That's why he'd kept the lights off, yet anxiousness settled deep in his stomach.

He found his room and slipped in, turning the lock as soon as the door closed on his back. He waited and listened. One heartbeat. Another. Then another. But there was no floorboard creaking nor breathing where none should be. He moved swiftly through the room, checking inside the cupboard and under the bed. When he found no one and nothing out of order, he allowed himself to relax.

Victor opened his pack. He put a small caliber gun in

the nightstand—it had taken a lot of paperwork after he'd left the military service to get a permit—and his knife in its sheath under the cushion. There had been no direct indication from Stephen that there would be trouble, but he'd learned it was better to be prepared from the beginning. Then he walked over to the window and propped it open. He breathed in and out and slipped into the bed. The sound of the waves lulled him. Seconds later, he was fast asleep.

For a moment, Thoma hesitated to set foot into his own home, then he scolded himself. The rest of his day had been peaceful. Clair had been kind enough to bring his dinner to the bookstore. That had allowed him to keep reading and slowly unwind. Now everything came flooding back. The calm mood that had surrounded him when he'd set out for the night evaporated once he remembered his guest.

The hallway was dark, and no lights shone from under doors. Thoma stretched his senses into the space, and a disturbance in the fabric of magic that shrouded the inn indicated another being was nearby. His ancestors' ghosts leaned in, waiting and whispering, uncomfortably close. Thoma made a small warding gesture to send them away. They resisted, persistent, until they finally dissipated. He made a mental note to tell Old Man Nathaniel to check the general wards. The ghosts were becoming too feisty.

Thoma carefully felt his way forward. He knew the house like the inside of his pockets, but he couldn't see a damn thing. It'd been different when he'd been out in the water. It was the same darkness, inky and all-encompassing, yet under the waves, he had never hesitated, his natural instinct as a selkie guiding him safely through the lightless currents.

He turned up the second set of stairs and waited on the half-landing. No one moved. There was no light, no sound; no shadows reaching for him. Thoma shook himself out of his disquiet and went all the way up, opening the only door at the top of the last flight of stairs.

A long time ago, the attic had been transformed into living quarters for the innkeeper who guarded the place. Now, the whole attic was his domain. It had a small kitchen that seldom saw use, a generous bedroom, a cozy living room, and a bath. The bath was the best thing, a free-standing claw-footed bathtub made of white enamel. It was beautiful. After a long day like this, he would usually marinate in the hot water and read another novel.

Tonight, he was too tired even for a shower. He changed and crawled into bed. The ghosts came back, hovering and whispering. They never fully formed—they couldn't. They were just imprints of the people who had once lived here and on the island, all tied to his family. There was no formula as to who remained as a ghost and who went over, but over the centuries, they had grown in numbers. Old Man Nathaniel reformed the wards every year at the winter and summer solstices. But in the last years, the ghosts had pushed and prodded against the barrier, wanting to be heard—wanting to be there, to follow Thoma around.

When he'd pointed them out to Nathaniel, the old man had only shaken his head and told Thoma that he was imagining things.

Thoma was very sure he wasn't. They'd grown to a critical mass and were now pushing beyond their realm.

He made a strong warding gesture, laying all his intent for peace and quiet into it. It hovered between him and his metaphysical guests until they reluctantly withdrew, taking Thoma's last bit of energy with them. He was out before he could even take his hand down.

Chapter 3

THE PERSISTENT CRY of a seagull woke Victor. He stared at the ceiling wondering whom he'd followed home last night and how many drinks had been involved. Another cry and the truth came slowly back. There were no seagulls in the city. He hadn't visited a bar and picked up some stranger for a fumble in the dark—a fact which was only marginally better than being stuck on this island.

His phone showed a cheery six o'clock and no reception bars. He peeled himself out of bed and changed into his running gear. Soon after leaving the military, it had become clear that a workout regimen would be the only thing to keep him remotely sane. So he took up the gym as any stereotypical ex-military retiree did. Running, too—there was something comforting in the constant movement. The world turned quiet and everything seemed possible.

When he stepped out of the room, the quality in the air had shifted compared to the previous evening. He hadn't heard Thoma come up, but Victor knew that the innkeeper was back. There was a rumbling under the surface, but the shadows had kept their peace yesterday, so Victor let them be.

Outside, the day had cropped up to be a beautiful one, a powder-blue sky with the odd white cloud. The air was crisp and fresh with the underlying tang of salt and fish.

A path led to the side of the inn, along the cliff wall, probably leading back to the village via the coastline. Victor's feet pounded across it, every step vibrating through him. There was a short, awkward moment, as always, before he found the correct rhythm, but once he hit it, he was flying. A few sheep raised their heads, eyeing him suspiciously with beady eyes, before returning to the more important grass before them. After a few miles, he reached another opening in the cliffs leading down to a small beach littered with pebbles made smooth and round from the tidewater. Victor stopped and looked toward the soft waves, the water coming in and pulling back in almost lazy, beckoning movements. Once more, a seagull squawked. Its call was answered by a gaggle of other gulls, drifting farther and farther away. Victor toed off his trainers and peeled his socks off, then stepped onto the beach, pebbles dislodging in a soft *clack-clack*. He walked to the water's edge. The water lapped at his feet. It was ice cold, and yet the constant shifting rhythm was soothing.

Victor wanted to step farther into it, just a few more steps, and yet he was rooted to the spot, his muscles straining against the will to move. He kneeled, his fingers sinking into the clear water. This was okay. This he could do. But when he looked up and across the gray, murky water, a shiver ran down his back. He felt the water rise in his lungs. The panic. The confusion over which way was up and which was down. His hands stretching through darkness to what he believed was the light and catching nothing...

Victor rose, turned, and walked back to his shoes. He cleaned his feet as best as he could, then slipped both his socks and shoes back on. The sun was warm on his skin, but he was chilled to his bones. He looked down the winding path and caught glimpses of the houses' roofs. He turned back to the inn, suppressing the feeling that he was still running away.

As Victor tried to slip back into his room, Thoma came down the stairs yawning and scratching his head. He had a pillow crease on his cheek and smelled of seawater and seaweed with the same burned-off edge that Victor had noticed yesterday. He stopped when he saw Victor, his brow creasing in confusion, as if he was unsure what Victor was doing here.

Then he sighed. "Coffee will be ready in a few minutes. Scrambled eggs good enough?"

Victor nodded, and Thoma hurried down the last flight of stairs. The smell of the sea lingered and, for once, it didn't make Victor nauseous.

Ten minutes later, Victor stumbled freshly showered into the dining room. A big pot of coffee was already waiting. The room had another door on the right side. It was open and showed a glimpse of an old, but clean, kitchen. Thoma was tending to a pan, humming a melody Victor didn't know. Not that he was versed in the current state of pop culture. While deployed, nothing reached them aside from the odd tune or craze. After his return, he didn't pay much attention, more concerned with earning enough money to put food in his mouth and a roof over his head. His heritage always caught up with him.

Victor took the cup into his massive hands and sipped. It was strong, but Victor savored the caffeine burst. The bitter liquid rolled over his tongue and chased the last tendrils of fatigue away. He spotted the check-in form and had just filled it out when Thoma stepped through the door, two plates in his hands. Crispy bacon, fresh toast with soft butter, and fluffy scrambled eggs. Victor's stomach growled on cue, and the corners of Thoma's mouth twitched.

They didn't speak while eating. What was there to say, anyway? Victor subtly tried to sniff out more of that strange, burned smell. There was a memory attached to it. He was sure he'd smelled it before, or at least something like it. But he couldn't pinpoint it.

"You'll stay out or in today?" Thoma wasn't looking at him. He'd uttered the question to his plate.

"I want to see if I can conclude my business today."

Thoma nodded and then took a sip from his mug. He looked out the window behind Victor, his eyes faraway. The smell of the sea suddenly became stronger. Victor had no clue what kind of heritage ran in Thoma's veins, so maybe he was, indeed, looking into another place or time, or even both.

A witch had told Victor once that the mighty spells of old still existed, those that had shaped the world they lived in, but nobody was willing to pay the terrible price they demanded. They'd said that the gods went extinct because of those spells.

"We can take lunch at the bookstore."

Victor blinked at him.

Thoma looked as surprised as Victor felt.

Intrigued, Victor settled on a short "Okay."

Thoma stood, gathered the dishes, and disappeared

into the kitchen. Victor retreated at the sound of porcelain being put a bit too forcefully into a sink.

Back upstairs, Victor checked the time. Half past seven. Checking the post office would be the first point on his agenda, and regardless of what occurred, he would have nothing else to do. Exploring the island looked better and better. He turned and went back into the dining room, knocking at the door to the kitchen.

Thoma startled.

"Yes?"

"Where does the were settlement start?"

Thoma squinted at him. "Why?"

"I'd like to stay clear of them."

Thoma studied him as if trying to figure him out. Best of luck on that. Then he shrugged. "They have wards up, and shields. You will know when you're too close."

"Is the mountain range their territory?"

Thoma shook his head. His hands worked the dishes in the sink, his movements fluid, as if he'd never done anything else. "No, it isn't, but they cluster at its feet. If you keep to the north side, you should be able to avoid them." He started scrubbing a pan. "Anything else?"

"No." And Victor turned to go.

He went back upstairs, got his smaller pack ready, and set out. Something pulled him back to the inn the moment he set his feet outside, but Victor resisted and soldiered on.

He had the sinking feeling that this mission was a terrible idea.

THOMA HAD KNOWN the moment Victor left the house. It was as if Victor had taken something with him. But it didn't make sense. Whatever it was hadn't been there before, so there was nothing for Thoma to miss.

Done with the kitchen, he grabbed the check-in form and filed it dutifully in the correct folder, which had been empty so far, and then left the inn to tend to the store.

He exhaled when the bookstore door closed behind him with a tinkle and the smell of his books welcomed him like an old friend. He had no clue why he'd made the offer for lunch. It had slipped out, as if for a moment he'd been possessed by someone else.

Thoma paused at the thought. No, the ghosts couldn't do that. They had no power. Not like that.

Thoma wanted to phone Clair and lament about what had happened, but she'd only laugh at him and tell him he'd done it because he wanted to "climb that hunk like a tree." She wasn't incorrect, exactly, yet he also didn't want an entanglement. What he did want was to be left alone. He had to rebuild his life into something comfortable and solid, and finally overcome the rage that bubbled up whenever he looked at one of his cousins or Old Man Nathaniel.

"I am fine" was his mantra when he woke in the morning, when he went out for the day, when he skittered around the wolves and the other residents of the island, and when he went to bed at night. Now Victor was throwing Thoma's tenacious hold on this illusion into jeopardy with his sheer presence alone. It wasn't good. It was terrible, and Thoma hated him for it.

He phoned Clair to tell her to add another sandwich to his usual order, and then, remembering who his guest for lunch was, told her to add two more and a side of chips.

Clair answered with a long moment of silence and then a cackle that could raise the dead.

Not that Clair actually could. She was a fae, but unlike her brothers and sisters who had left for the mainland and the court, teetering on that morally gray line, she was all sunshine and genuine care. Clair's mother had left after she was born. Maybe she'd known her daughter would be useless for the court of the wild. That there wasn't an ounce of mischievousness or careless cruelty in her. Everybody loved Clair, and Thoma was lucky enough to count her as a friend. His only friend.

Her father, Per, had watched their close friendship with narrowed eyes and a frown between his brows until Thoma had found the courage to take him to the side and explain he'd never be interested in her like *that*. That assurance had calmed Per down. When Thoma had explained the same thing to Clair, she'd only smiled and told him she'd always known because her magic, as latent as it was, had no effect on him. So, it was as clear to her as if he'd screamed it in the middle of the village courtyard.

Whenever she brought food and she had the time, she would stay and they'd talk about nothing in particular or about gossip she'd picked up at the pub. Never anything malicious. Just the day by day of the people, allowing him to be part of the community while he hovered at the fringes.

Thoma tidied up the crime section and then dusted all the cases. Not that they had gathered much. The day proved to be as uneventful as the day before, and the day before, and the day before. He clung stubbornly to the notion that this was all he'd ever wanted.

When the church tower announced twelve o'clock, the bell over the door jingled. Thoma's mouth ran dry as he looked over. Victor filled out the doorframe quite nicely. His heart gave a double beat, and he remembered, suddenly, that wolves could smell emotions: fear; anxiety; arousal...

Desperately attempting to get himself under control, his gaze fell onto the sandwiches Clair had brought over not even half an hour ago. She'd tried to loiter around to catch another glimpse of Victor, but Thoma had pointed out that the pub was busy at this time of day. Her parting gaze had been anything but kind. Thinking about it helped Thoma finally calm down.

"Right on time," Thoma said, his eyes still on the sandwiches.

Victor huffed and came closer. All of space-time seemed to bend around him. Thoma was hyper aware of where the were was. The whole shop hummed restlessly. Thoma walked around the counter, and Victor stopped on the other side. He had the same cocky grin he'd had when they'd met for the first time. Then, and now, it enraptured Thoma. It wasn't arrogance, rather surety that Victor knew who he was and how he appeared to other people. Thoma wondered what Victor's actual job entailed. He'd wondered then, as well, but they'd been too preoccupied for a heart-to-heart.

This line of thinking wasn't helping.

"I'm always on time," Victor said in that deep rumbling voice that went to all kinds of different parts of Thoma.

Thoma rolled his eyes, desperately trying to play nonchalant. *Fake it till you make it.* He pointed at the sandwiches and two ale bottles. "Choose whichever you like best. I also had Clair bring a side of chips, and she threw in the ale. We aren't allowed to tell Per, though."

Victor snapped a salute and hopped onto the counter.

Thoma narrowed his eyes, but Victor ignored him and inspected the packages before settling on the ones with the cold meat cuts. Thoma suppressed a smile. There was a vegetarian percentage among the wolves, but it was lower than the percentage of the overall population, and veganism was non-existent. It was unclear whether it was a biological, psychological, or cultural thing. The remaining sandwich had grilled vegetables and cheese, which suited Thoma quite well. He grabbed the package that Victor was offering and tucked in.

When they were done sipping their ales, Thoma scrambled for something to say. "So, how is the business going?"

Victor let his bottle sink and sighed. "I came to get a package that's being kept in the post office. I thought I got lucky when I found the door open this morning, but the only employee there threw me out and told me to come back when it was 'officially' open." He air-quoted the word "officially."

Thoma frowned. He knew the post employee; they only had one. Jonathan was an easy-going wolf, one of the island wolves born and bred. He always wanted to help. He'd trained on the mainland before returning and taking over for the too-old man who had run the office for almost fifty years before. The old man had left for the mainland to live with relatives.

"Was it a blond man with freckles?"

"Aye."

It was Jonathan. His behavior didn't make sense.

"Why are you asking?"

"Never knew anyone Jonathan would throw out of the post when it was open." Thoma spread his fingers to dip up the last crumbs. "Shows what I know." But he kept frowning.

Victor shrugged. With him sitting on the counter, he almost looked like a schoolboy, shy and approachable. "I'll just return when it is open."

"You're confident he has the package."

Victor took another sip and then smiled. Thoma was glad that he had his hands on the counter; his knees suddenly turned to jelly. "If not, I'll find it." Cocky bastard.

Had Thoma thought Victor wasn't arrogant? Well, scratch that.

"Have fun then." He waved his hand magnanimously.

Victor grinned and leaned his head back to catch the last drop of the cider. Then he hopped down and looked at the sandwich paper and bottles.

"Leave it here, I'll take it over for dinner."

"You'll eat in the pub today?"

Was he going to? Victor looked almost hopeful. Why was he doing this to himself? He should say no, and he should show Victor the door here and at the inn. He didn't do either of those things; he nodded instead.

Victor flashed him another of those easy smiles that did unspeakable things to Thoma's insides, then, with a "Will see you then," he was gone.

The bell tinkled cheerfully at his back. The bell had never been cheerful in all the time Thoma had worked at the shop.

Thoma buried his head in his arms and groaned. What was he getting himself into?

VICTOR LEFT THE bookstore in a good mood and checked the post office once more, but it was now dark and the door was locked. He sighed and looked around. People eyed him but didn't bother him. He could see one or two werewolves lurking around, probably ordered by Maxim to keep track of him. He resisted the urge to wave. Maybe he should take them on a hike tomorrow. Victor grinned at the thought of them huffing and puffing up the hill, trying to keep hidden and cursing the day Victor had set foot on the island.

He stuffed his hands in his pockets and looked back at the bookstore. Thoma wanted him. It had been clear as day, and yet Thoma hadn't given an inch. Victor had even hopped onto the counter like a teen boy, the wood groaning under his weight. But Thoma had stayed where he was, outside of Victor's personal space.

Victor wondered if Thoma was the man Victor thought he was. And, if so, why was he denying it? Was he so ashamed about what they had shared? Or was it something different? The mysterious stranger from three years ago and Thoma did share similarities, not that Victor and that man had talked much before they'd fallen into bed. But there was also that weird, off-putting smell. It hadn't been there before.

Victor stopped at the edge of the harbor overlooking the ocean. He checked his phone and found that out here, he could at least get one signal bar. He texted Stephen and let him know about the holdup.

Stephen's reply was swift.

Stephen
Keep me posted.
How is the island?

Victor
Not what I expected.

Stephen
How so?

> **Victor**
> Different vibe, ancient magic in the
> earth. Protected by the ocean.

Stephen
Expecting any dragons to slay?

> **Victor**
> Ha. Once was more than enough.

Stephen
Worried, Captain?

> **Victor**
> No, just lonely out here.

The next reply took longer. The dots of Stephen typing appeared and disappeared a few times.

Stephen
Come and find me when you are back.

Victor considered the answer. That would've been a given; he needed to hand the package over to get the payment. No, this was something different, something that hadn't quite been on his radar. In the military, they hadn't had much occasion to find release. Being gay and a were reduced the pool of potential partners tremendously. He and Stephen had come to an arrangement then but hadn't rekindled it after they both left. He contemplated it. They'd never work as an actual couple, but at least he could forget about his feelings for a while.

Victor
All right.

Stephen
See you then.

Victor pocketed his phone and settled on a nearby bench. The sun stood high in the sky, and a few gulls flew lazy circles under it. For miles there was nothing but water. He closed his eyes and leaned his head back. The sounds of the village, people talking and laughing, the distant smell of someone cooking, music from an open window, the soft breeze, he let these impressions of normal life flow around him, soothe him. The city was angry, fast paced, and cutthroat. Never stopping. Never calming. The island was like a lazy roll, soft and gentle. The magic permeated every inch of the soil, guarding every movement above it in a sleepy drowsiness.

A shift to his side, and Victor opened one eye, studying his sudden bench guest.

It was an old man, older than the captain of the ferry. His face was lined with deep folds, giving him a haggard look. His skin was nearly white and his ice-blue eyes piercing. He had a passing resemblance to Thoma; it was in the lines of his jaw, the shape of the eyes, and his wild hair. The same suspicious glint in his gaze, looking deeper and deeper, hell-bent on sniffing out all of Victor's soul's secrets.

"When will you be gone?" His voice sounded like pebbles grinding on each other in the water, cracking and clacking. It seemed to be the question of the week. Everyone wanted him off the island as fast as possible. Victor watched the old man through one eye. He wasn't a were. At least not a werewolf. He was not fae, nor troll, nor any creature Victor had met on his travels. There was a faint resemblance to a water creature—a nymph he'd met down in the Riverlands. But he wasn't like the nymph had been, either. And yet he was magic. Strong and very old magic.

"When the ferry captain returns."

The old man nodded and turned his face to the sea, squinting into the waters and then raising his head and watching the sea gulls. "It'll be a while, then. This storm is relentless."

Victor followed his gaze, but there wasn't even the smidge of darkness on the horizon.

The old man chuckled. "It will come."

The old man was probably right. Out in the desert, Victor'd learned to smell the oncoming storms on the wind, and if the old man really had a connection to the water, he would know. At least he was old enough to have learned to read the pattern.

"When you go, will you take him with you?"

Victor's mind instantly leaped to one person. "Who?"

"You know who I mean. You already met, on the other side of the sea. Through that, it would be possible to take him with you."

That cleared that up. Thoma was his mysterious stranger, the one he'd been pining after since he'd been left alone in that hotel room. While it had been somewhat expected that the then-stranger had left without a word the next morning, Victor had still tried to find him. But no one had known who he was or from whence he had come. So

Victor had waited, and searched, and hoped.

And all the time, Thoma had been here.

"I don't think he wants to come." Otherwise Thoma wouldn't have denied knowing him.

Victor looked over, but the old man was gone. He contemplated returning to the bookstore and demanding to know what game Thoma was playing—but everyone had secrets, hadn't they?

WHEN THE BELL tinkled a bit later, Thoma almost thought that Victor had forgotten something. It wasn't his guest filling the door again, however, but Old Man Nathaniel, watching him out of those deep blue eyes. When Thoma had been younger, he'd thought those eyes were the sea and the sky mixed into one. Never angry. Never stormy. Always soothing.

As an adult, he'd learned better.

Old Man Nathaniel was the head of the family, and he made himself known when needed.

They stared at each other before Thoma made a beckoning motion, allowing Old Man Nathaniel entry. Not that he needed it, but it was courtesy, aligned with some false sense of propriety.

"Good that you've come. Someone needs to check the wards on the inn; the ancestors are getting feisty."

Old Man Nathaniel raised an eyebrow. "The inn has no ghosts. I've told you many times."

Thoma set his jaw. "I never called them ghosts, only ancestors. Call them what you want, but they are talking in the shadows, and I want them to stop."

Old Man Nathaniel watched him.

Thoma knew he wasn't believed; no one believed him. He hadn't always been able to sense the murky darkness spilling around them—not malicious, but also not friendly. They just were—controlling the energy surrounding the land the inn sat on. And they liked to be in control. The wards, even if they weren't designed for the ancestors specifically, kept them reigned in, at least enough that Thoma could live with their constant presence.

Old Man Nathaniel sighed. "I'll make sure the wards are solid."

"Thank you," Thoma said tersely, and waited. Old Man Nathaniel never made social calls just to talk about the weather and how his day had been.

"Will you go when your guest goes?"

Thoma scrunched his brows. That hadn't been a question he'd expected. "Why should I?" Why was Old Man Nathaniel bringing that up, and why now?

"Because he is the one you bonded with on the mainland. The island will accept that." Old Man Nathaniel said it matter-of-factly, as if he were indeed talking about the weather.

Thoma pressed his fingernails into the wood of the counter. "There was no bond." And even if there had been, there would definitely be no bond now.

"I smell him on you."

"He's staying at the inn, and he is a wolf, and wolves smell." Thoma tried to keep his emotions in check. By the glint in the old man's eyes, he was failing.

"Why do you want me gone?" It wasn't the first time Old Man Nathaniel had brought up the possibility of Thoma leaving; shortly after Thoma had returned from the mainland, begging for a place to stay, the old man had given him one, but he'd also made it clear that Thoma should return to the mainland—his ancestors' home wasn't his home anymore.

"You aren't *of* here anymore. You never have been." That hurt. And it made him furious.

"Out."

A flash in those ice-blue eyes. A terrible storm. Old Man Nathanial didn't budge.

"I said, *out*," Thoma repeated.

It was a terrible choice he was making, but he'd lost the will to care. The magic of the land obeyed, and Old Man Nathaniel didn't fight it. He was pushed out the door, which closed behind him with a *bang*.

Thoma stared after where the old man had gone, then he walked to the door, flipped the sign to "Closed," and turned the lock. He slumped between his bookshelves, out of view, letting the sun sink and the shadows grow and stretch, chasing the last sun rays away.

His parents had come from far away, they'd settled here and brought him with them. They'd loved and cared for him until they went out into the sea and never returned. Old Man Nathaniel had raised him, allowed Thoma to make his home here, even gave him command of the magic of the land, but it had always been clear that this wasn't his ancestral home. That he was, and would always be, a stranger.

THE DAY PLAYED out like the afternoon before had. Victor checked the post office, but it never opened again. He kept an eye out for any of the were, but his detail kept away and didn't interfere. From time to time, Victor thought he saw Maxim's second lurking in his peripheral vision, but when he looked closer, Trevor wasn't there.

When the evening came, he settled in the pub at the same table as the previous night. Clair greeted him with a smile and brought him the same cider. She also informed him that today's dinner would be shepherd's pie. He nodded, and waited.

And waited.

And waited.

When Clair brought the pie, he touched her arm. "Was Thoma already here?"

Clair cocked her head to the side, considering him. "I'm not sure he'll be coming."

"He said he'd eat here today." He sounded like a petulant child and barely resisted the urge to cross his arms.

Clair shrugged and moved on.

Victor stared down at his food, not really hungry anymore.

He'd wanted to talk to Thoma. Granted, maybe the noisy and nosy environment of a pub wasn't the best for a heart-to-heart, but he'd hoped that it at least presented neutral ground. Something was wrong. Something had happened after Thoma had sneaked out of that hotel room three years ago. Victor had gone over the night often enough, trying to find a point when he may have forced Thoma into something, pushed him too far, or not listened. But he hadn't found anything. No fissure of an emotion out of place, a smell better left alone, nothing. The night was a hazy memory of pleasure and emotional highs he'd barely been allowed to feel since he had been a teen.

The military had burned the concept of happiness out of him, but that night had seared it right back into every single cell.

He forced the thoughts away and mechanically ate the

pie and drank the cider, and when Clair inquired about both, he nodded and smiled and said all the right words.

Outside, his feet put him directly in front of the bookstore, the sign reading "Seaman and Son, Bookstore" almost weathered away. The window frames and the door had the same blue color as the inn. There was no light, and as he tried the handle, just to check, it was locked. He stepped back and stared at the sign. It didn't magically change to tell him what to do. That kind of thing only happened in books and TV shows. In the real world, magic was a wild force, all-encompassing and devastating, set by intention and will. With the right emotion, even a magical being with a mere flicker of power could move mountains and shatter the moon. Victor looked up into the sky. The moon hung pale and silvery, the spiderweb of cracks on its surface visible even from here. It hung in delicate balance as if one touch could shatter it.

He let his eyes drift down again and caught a light in the post office. Another chance, then.

The wind picked up as he walked over, clouds gathering on the horizon. Victor licked his lips. A storm was brewing. He had no experience with the sea to use to determine when it would hit the island, but he knew he should hurry.

The post office door was half open, so he pushed it all the way and knocked on the frame. The same man— Jonathan, Thoma had called him—was hunched over behind the counter, muttering and opening and closing drawers. His hair was in disarray, and he had dark rings under his eyes. At Victor's entry, his head snapped up, a flash of fear flitting over his face.

"You again!"

Victor held up his hands in a warding-off gesture. "I just need the package."

"You'll get yours as every other person does, when I open." He accentuated the last words.

"But you are open right now."

Jonathan snarled. He actually snarled. His thin body produced a surprisingly deep sound.

"Calm your horses."

But all he got was another snarl. Victor moved backward, out of the office and down the steps, never moving his eyes away from Jonathan.

Jonathan followed him, closed the door with a bang, and turned the lock pointedly.

Victor sighed, and someone snickered to his left. He turned and found Maxim's second-in-command standing a few paces away. His eyes glowed with malice; he was itching for a fight. Victor could smell it on him, the same way he could smell the tangy sea and the incoming rain. The last two days had thrown Victor, and he needed a way to lose the restless energy that had accumulated in his veins. A fuck would be one way, a fight another. But the wolf, even if he got on Victor's nerves, wasn't the best punching bag...or fuck buddy. Trevor wanted to throw the first punch. Victor wasn't sure why he was so desperate for it, but he didn't want to give him the satisfaction.

No, Trevor was better left alone. Victor threw him a sharp smile and then turned and walked in the opposite direction, ignoring the itchy feeling between his shoulder blades.

The moment he stepped out from between the houses, heading in the direction of the dirt road, the heavens opened and the rain poured down. He looked up. The storm had come faster than he'd have thought possible. Heavy, rolling clouds blotted out the moon, lightning flashed, and then deep thunder rolled over the land.

Victor stopped, and for a moment, he lived in it. Something was happening, something he couldn't put his finger on. In the distance, the inn was dark. No light, just dark holes on a white façade.

And yet it was calling him, beckoning him, siren-like.

Victor went willingly.

THOMA LET THE mounting crescendo of the music float around him. The falling drums, the desperate piano, the orchestra preparing for something out of reach for a mere mortal, higher and higher, wilder and wilder, until it all came together, rearing up for one last attempt to hold forever and then falling away until nothing was left but emptiness.

A breeze, pushed in through the windows by the oncoming storm, caressed Thoma's face. He'd thrown all the windows open. The curtains billowed in the wind like the ghosts who stalked the halls. With his naked feet firmly planted on the wooden floor of the living room, he raised his hands with the rising music and let them dance. A storm of instruments and thundering musical notes—a matching storm inside him.

The moment the requiem choir started, Victor crossed the threshold of the inn's main door as if he was starting his own funeral mass. His own downhill path. It was ironic how fitting it felt. Thoma sensed Victor shifting through the halls, the fabric of the inn pulling itself aside to let him through, until he stood in the open door of the living room, a mountain of a presence. The singer rose above them, her sweet voice filling the room, Thoma, and the ocean outside.

Lightning flashed. The thunder rolled through his bones as the choir rose anew.

"I'm broken." Thoma stopped the fluttering motions but didn't turn. Had Victor even heard him over the loud music?

"No one is broken."

Thoma snorted. "I'm only half of what I once was. Left to be nothing, I'm tolerated by my elders and despised by my peers."

"Thoma." Just a name. It described everything so clearly and spoke of all he was and wasn't anymore. Of all the hopes and dreams he'd once had, now ripped away.

"What do you want?" He was exhausted from hiding, from living. He was tired of standing alone in a room while the storm drove the waves against the cliff, nearly to the edge of the living room. One day the ocean would claim the whole inn—the whole island. Thoma hoped it was soon.

Victor came closer, wading through the ghosts he couldn't see or feel. No one could. Thoma's cousins mocked him about them. Clair pitied him for them.

The pressure of the music mounted, and fingers touched his shoulders the moment it crashed down. He allowed himself to be turned around and pressed close, as if the storm and the music had sapped all his energy out.

The next track.

Eyes dark as the night, hungry and powerful, stared him down. "I just want you." And while the music thundered on, Victor raised Thoma's chin and kissed him.

There was a split second during which he wondered if he should fight it, wrench himself away, and banish Victor from the inn, or even the island. His breath hitched, and Victor's tongue took the invitation.

Everything was driven away.

Thoma gave in. He gave in to everything while the storm raged on. The rain was probably ruining the parquet. The curtains were already a soggy mess. But for once, Thoma didn't care. Didn't care but for the powerful naked body over him and expert fingers touching every inch of his skin, reaching deep inside him, claiming him until he had nothing left to be claimed and then giving it back in one blinding, drawn-out flash of molten liquid fire that flooded his veins and mind and tingled down to his nerve endings.

After, they lay together, catching their breath. Victor didn't let him go, and Thoma wasn't sure whether he welcomed the continued closeness or was repelled by it. Without making a decision, he let Victor clean them both up and let himself be gathered and cuddled. Under them, in the living room, the last song in his playlist fell away. Soon only the wind remained. For once, Thoma could live with it.

THUNDERING OF A different kind woke Victor. Disoriented, he groaned and wondered what was going on. It took him a full minute to realize that someone must be hammering at the inn door. Thoma stirred in his arms, groaned as well, and flopped to the other side.

Victor allowed himself a smile, then heaved out of the bed, grabbed jeans and a T-shirt, and raked his fingers through his hair as he walked downstairs.

He threw the door open just as their early-morning guest was about to lay into it again. For a second Per, the pub owner, blinked owlishly, fist raised awkwardly in midair.

Recognition entered his gaze, and he straightened up. "Where is Thoma?"

"I'm here," came the rough voice from behind Victor. Thoma looked ethereal in the dimly lit hallway. With his nearly white skin, ice-blue eyes, and dark hair, he looked out of this world. Like a member of the wild court, or even beyond them, an old god. As if he wasn't supposed to be here.

"I'm only half of what I once was."

Victor wondered what he'd meant.

"What is going on?" Thoma stepped up to Victor, who made space but did not leave him alone, intent on protecting him, ready to secure the premises and Thoma.

Per's eyes flicked from Thoma to him and back and then he exhaled. "It's Jonathan. They found him dead, and they say your guest murdered him."

Chapter 4

"I did what?"

Victor looked offended, almost comically so, and Thoma had a hard time suppressing a smile. But Per had his eyes fixed on Victor, a gravity to his gaze that sobered Thoma right up again.

"Where is he?" Thoma asked.

"At the post office."

"Has Maxim been informed?" Jonathan was a wolf; this could be a wolf matter.

Per nodded, his gaze moving to him. "He is waiting for you."

Of course he was. Thoma sighed, and Victor looked at him, surprised. Thoma hadn't had the energy to explain himself or how this island worked. There was a dead body, and he hadn't had any coffee—this day was shaping up to be a bad one.

"You can tell him that we're coming."

"But—"

"Per, the body won't walk away. I just rolled out of bed. I need coffee before I do anything for anyone. We'll be there shortly."

"Maxim won't like it," Per tried to interject again.

"I don't care." Maxim had known him and the island long enough to know how this worked.

Per shrugged and turned, walking back down the small path to the village. Thoma closed the door and let his head rest against it, allowing himself a moment. His mind was spinning. This wasn't good. If Jonathan had really been murdered, then the killer was on or close to the island. The inhabitants were already pointing their fingers at Victor, and Thoma had hoped—nothing, he'd hoped nothing, he realized. Victor was bound to go in a few days, leaving the island behind and, by extension, Thoma.

"Thoma."

"What?" Thoma snapped.

He hadn't the mental capacity to read the emotions flashing over Victor's face before Victor settled on something neutral and asked, "Coffee?"

"I...yes." Thoma looked down at his own clothing. The shirt was buttoned wrong, and he was missing a sock. He felt gritty; was this a prolonged nightmare he'd yet to wake up from? "I will shower, and then we need to go."

TWENTY MINUTES LATER, they finally pushed through the crowd that had formed in front of the post office. Victor hadn't said a word since they left the inn. Thoma welcomed the silence. His own thoughts were a mangled mess. He nodded absentmindedly at the two wolves guarding the entrance, then slipped in. Victor followed slowly, cautiously. The energy of the crowd members had changed when they'd recognized them. They weren't angry yet, but they were suspicious. Holding their breaths.

The post office looked the same as always. The dark wooden counter, the faded green carpet, and the old sorting boxes gave the interior a timeless feeling. It looked the same as it had when Thoma was a small boy and came here with his parents. Modern technology hadn't found its way inside, aside from the ceiling light. The folks on the island said the old magic that ran through the ocean prevented even a network cable from being laid down. Thoma knew it was the island itself that didn't approve of such frivolities.

Nothing seemed to be disturbed or out of place. Before the counter lay the crumpled body of Jonathan, his eyes dead, Maxim crouching over him. From his position, Thoma saw a nasty-looking gash on Jonathan's temple. Blood had pooled under his head in a now-black stain.

The leader of the wolves rose when they stepped in. He nodded at them. "Thoma."

"Maxim."

"What is he doing here?" Trevor's growl from behind the counter asked. He pointed at Victor.

Maxim sighed. "Down, Trevor. Victor, you were seen arguing with the deceased."

Victor crossed his arms and shrugged. "I looked in after I was at the pub and before I returned to the inn. There was light and the door was open, so I thought he might be amicable and hand the package over."

"And he didn't."

"He threw me out, closed the door, and locked it, and I went away. As you would be able to confirm." His eyes flashed, and Trevor snarled.

"Trevor, is that true? Was Jonathan alive when Victor walked away?"

Trevor mumbled something that almost sounded like a confirmation.

"So, he was killed?" Thoma interjected, walking closer to the corpse.

"You tell me," Maxim said evenly, his eyes now on Thoma.

"Chief, that is mumbo jumbo."

"Thoma," Maxim said and stepped to the side.

Thoma rolled his eyes and crouched in Maxim's place. He closed his eyes and spread his hands, holding them an inch over the skin. There wasn't much to sense. The life energy was long gone, always dissipating the fastest, and there wasn't any magic left behind to properly read, even as the island pushed her own magic into his hands to help him. No, Jonathan hadn't been struck by a spell or a potion or a curse. And yet an imprint of bloodthirst and anger remained, mixing with the faint tendrils of panic and horror.

He stood. "He didn't die peacefully, but there was no magic involved."

Maxim growled and pinched the bridge of his nose. "Doc will take a look. You're welcome to send one of your own."

Thoma shook his head. That wouldn't be necessary. "Old Man Nathaniel trusts you. You'll tell us the truth. As it was promised."

"As it was promised," Maxim repeated. A soft chime answered their promises, the contract the sides had formed a long time ago.

There was a shift next to Thoma. "Yes?"

"I'm sorry to be callous, but was my package found?"

"Eager to get away?" Thoma had only wanted to think those words, but they slipped out. Victor went very still, and then his shoulders dropped as he'd lost a fight. Thoma didn't want to examine that feeling too closely. Some things weren't meant to be.

"We'll check the storage to see if this was a burglary gone

wrong," Maxim said easily. "Was it addressed to you?"

"It should have been."

Maxim nodded. "We'll let you know, if or when we find it."

Victor inclined his head in a thank-you gesture, and then he turned sharply on his heels and walked out. Thoma didn't follow him with his eyes, but he felt the pull to do so. A headache formed at the base of his skull. He didn't want to deal with this, whatever had happened to Jonathan and a now sulky Victor. He wanted...fuck, what he wanted. His own island probably. His eyes sought out Maxim's. "I'll leave the rest to you, then."

Maxim nodded and stepped close, his mouth nearly brushing Thoma's ear as he murmured, "He smells like death." Then he passed Thoma, shouting for Doc and at the people outside to get moving again.

Thoma looked at the body. A death too young. He sighed and threw Trevor a last look—he was watching Thoma with narrowed eyes—and then turned and stepped outside himself.

The crowd had dispersed, but stretching above, as if to mock him, was a clear blue sky.

As HE WALKED down the path, Thoma wondered briefly where Victor had disappeared to. There was no escape off the island, at least not for a wolf. Thoma walked in the direction of the inn and then veered onto a different path, leading him through the cliffs to a small opening. It was only visible if one knew it was there. He went down to the pebbled beach. He could've gone to the one directly by the inn, but he wanted to make sure that Victor didn't see him.

He toed off his shoes, slipped off his socks, and then walked down, the stones making a soft *clack, clack.* Welcoming their smooth and almost velvety feeling, he stepped into the water and waited. The waves licked at his calves, wetting his trouser legs, beckoning him to come deeper, to return to the sea, to dance once more in the waves and play with the fish. Thoma set his jaw against the hollow feeling threatening to swallow him whole. The resentment churned in his stomach. Thoma wondered if he'd ever lose that feeling entirely, or if time would just temper it. Would it always remain under the surface, ready to spill out again?

"I'm broken."

"No one is broken."

A head appeared, rising from the surface, round and glistening with water, dark eyes watching him.

"We need to talk."

The seal bobbed under and surfaced closer to Thoma, and then an old man walked out of the ocean. Old Man Nathaniel was the leader of the selkie tribe that had been living around the island since Thoma was young; he'd probably been the leader for many decades before then, too. He and his tribe were the true masters of this rock; the wolves were only tolerated.

More seals bobbed their heads out of the water, never emerging farther than their noses, beady eyes watching. Thoma recognized some of them, his distant cousins. His own family was long gone. His mother and father had come from a more northern tribe, Old Man Nathaniel had told him once, and they had settled here and then had died.

His cousins disapproved of him. A selkie should be in

the sea and didn't belong on the land.

"Speak, son."

Thoma sighed. "One of the wolves was killed. Jonathan, the wolf at the post office. Maxim is leading the investigation."

The old man studied him, looking deeper and deeper with those ice-blue eyes, fathomless like the deep sea. Thoma hated the feeling of being dissected layer by layer. "I'll ask the tribe who's been onshore. Keep me informed."

"Aye."

Old Man Nathaniel nodded and watched him a minute longer. He opened his mouth as if he wanted to say something, but he closed it again, then shook his head and turned back. He took a few steps and jumped once, and instead of a man, a seal flashed through the depths of water, leaping through the waves.

Thoma pressed down a flash of envy and made the trek back to the inn.

Victor walked as far as the harbor before he needed to sit down. Seeing the dead dredged up memories better left alone. He fumbled out his phone.

Victor
The post office boy is dead.

Stephen
Are you kidding me? Tell me you got
the damn package.

Victor
Working on it.

Stephen
Make it faster.

Victor
The ferry is still a few days out. Even
if I got it faster, I couldn't leave.

This morning he hadn't even wanted to leave, but now? Shit, this was getting more complicated by the minute.

Stephen
Do something or I will.

Victor snorted. "Good luck with that," he said into the air while putting the phone away.

If the package didn't appear over the day, he would ask Maxim to be allowed to search for it himself. And then? He would deliver it, get the money...and move on. That was what he'd always done. Move on. No one was waiting for him, and no one depended on him. Maybe he and Stephen could have something, but he knew it wouldn't be enough, it wouldn't be what he craved: that fabled connection that the weres called "the bond." Not like soulmates, but instead a closeness and a feeling of belonging.

"Eager to get away?"

Victor swallowed and looked over the too-calm water. Someone had bumped off the poor boy and the second-in-command Trevor seemed willing to pin it on him. Maxim not so much, at least not yet. Maybe his only saving grace. Hopefully Trevor would never take over the investigation.

Victor wondered what he'd done to the other were to warrant that kind of dedication. But sometimes someone just rubbed one the wrong way. Victor'd had his fair share of fights with those types. He normally avoided those who smelled wrong to him and gave off that weird vibe, that itch for a fight. They seldom extended the same courtesy to him.

Society did not look too favorably on his brand of were, and wolves who couldn't keep their instincts under control didn't help. Victor knew that control was hard to master; it was hard to not fall back on what they deemed to be instinct but were actually just poorly controlled habits. But it could be done.

A seal's head bobbed up, watching him with dark, knowing eyes. A second followed, and a third. They hovered, rising and falling with the water around them. A minute or two later, they submerged again and swam away, their gray-and-white bodies shadows under the surface.

Victor watched them go and wondered, not for the first time, if there lived here more magical creatures than just the weres on the island's far side.

Someone was in control of this land. He'd felt it. And it hadn't been Maxim.

Victor fiddled with his phone in his pocket, unsure what to do from here. He hated to wait for something to happen to him. But there was not much he could do until Maxim handed him the package and sent him on his merry way.

He considered going to the pub but scratched that out before the thought even finished. Victor had seen the gazes of the island people. Those were the same gazes bestowed upon him in and out of the military. He was a welcome fighter but not more. Suspicious, unsympathetic, they rejected everything about him. And yet he couldn't blame them; they had a dead body, and he was an outsider.

Victor rose and looked around. He found a small path that curved from the harbor through the grassy hills along the cliff line. This might be the path he'd jogged on. He stepped on it, hoping that it would lead him back to the inn without encountering anyone.

HE WASN'T SO lucky. Halfway down, Thoma appeared from between the cliffs and nearly ran him over.

"Sorry," Thoma said after avoiding the collusion.

Victor shook his head, and after making sure Thoma would stay on his feet, Victor stepped back. Everything in him screamed against doing it. He wanted to gather Thoma close and smooth out the worry lines that had formed between his brows and around the corners of his mouth.

Thoma was in a pensive mood.

"On the way to the inn?"

Thoma only nodded and didn't offer more.

Victor suppressed a sigh and started walking; Thoma fell into a step beside. Victor was sure Thoma didn't even realize he'd done so.

There was a heaviness to their silence that Victor didn't like.

"Eager to get away?"

He was and wasn't at the same time. He needed to get the job done; that was why he'd been hired, and he prided himself on always completing his missions as well as possible. It was only to a degree about the money; he'd accepted the job and he would do the job. His personal and professional pride were on the line.

And yet he'd wanted to return, figure something out, and then go from there, but one night hadn't seemed to make the same difference to Thoma as it had to Victor. He should have known better; Thoma had done the same thing three years ago.

They walked through the door, and Thoma got some rags to mop up the mess that had come through the open windows the previous night. Victor watched him for a second, wondering if he was welcome, before throwing caution to the wind and helping anyway.

After Thoma had put the last rag away, Victor, emboldened by having received no outward rejection, caught his hand. It was ice cold. Thoma looked at it, confused, and then his eyes traveled up Victor's arm until he looked Victor in the eyes, his gaze far away.

"Thoma."

"Let me go." The voice was mechanical.

Victor waited a beat longer, but Thoma didn't elaborate, so Victor did as requested.

Thoma cradled his wrist close, stepping back. "Don't touch me again." The same hollow voice.

"Last night—"

"Shouldn't have happened."

"But—"

"No!" The word echoed through the room and sank into the walls. There was skittering and scratching, and then the whispering began.

The walls were slowly moving closer.

Victor swallowed and held up his hands. "As you wish." He stepped back, turned, and walked up to his room.

For a moment, he waited, his feet braced, his hands lax at his side. But nothing happened, no attack came, no magic sought him out. He allowed himself to relax, sinking onto the floor cross-legged, burying his head in his hands.

Victor hadn't wanted to believe it, but they had shared something last night, just as they had the first night. And yet he wasn't welcome on this island or in Thoma's life.

It was time to let go of an impossible dream: the one where he was more than a monster that hunted other monsters.

THOMA BLINKED AT the door through which Victor had just left. He'd woken the ghosts, had put power into a simple "No." Had wielded the magic he had left because someone had touched him, had wanted to touch him, had held him close despite Thoma being as he was, only half of himself, a mere shadow of what he'd once been.

He swallowed.

Everything was just too much.

The spilled blood, the violence of the death, and the broken oath associated with it had made the land unhappy. Old Man Nathaniel had told him it was his job to make sure the land was happy. As a land-dweller, it was his role to communicate between the islanders and the ruling selkie. Last night he'd allowed himself to be selfish, to seek a smattering of happiness, and the land had paid the price.

His fingers danced over the nearby table.

The clock in the corner struck the hour.

The shadows slowly quieted down.

Nothing more happened, so they returned to biding their time, waiting.

Thoma shook his head and decided to make the trek down to the wolves' settlement.

WALKING THROUGH THE green meadows and small woods brought back memories. Thoma used to explore the land as he did the sea, always at his parents' side. After they'd gone, before he'd lost the other part of himself, he'd honored them by doing the same. Exploring where he hadn't before, dreaming of what lay beyond, and revisiting the places he'd once been, savoring the bittersweet memories. Old Man Nathaniel had called him a sentimental fool, and maybe he was one. But it'd brought him peace and happiness.

The wolves had settled an hour out from the village, at a small bay at the foot of the mountains. There had once been an older settlement there, long crumbled to dust, but it'd had enough material left that the wolves had been able to make use of it and build on top of the old foundations. The island had liked that, welcoming them, understanding their intention of being allowed to settle somewhere in peace.

The villagers had mumbled about it, but Old Man Nathaniel had set them straight. They were only tolerated; the true masters were still the selkies, and above them, the island had its own will.

A powerful will, currently trembling under his feet.

With every passing hour it would get worse, until the land would start to reject everyone who lived here. Ancient, powerful magic. Books told Thoma that there weren't many such places; trying to understand them had been what led him off the island in the first place— research, and wanting to understand the world he lived in and find other places like this and learn from them.

Instead, it'd led to his ruin and now he was as good as bound here. The only place he could see himself living.

Thoma waved at the two wolves who leaned casually at the entrance gate. They had rebuilt the wall that had once surrounded the smaller village, not to protect but to keep out those who might trespass accidentally. Wolves didn't like strangers sniffing around on their territory.

"Is Maxim in?" he called to Sal, a huge wolf currently doing some intricate woodwork.

Sal looked up, his eyes narrowing before amusement twinkled in them. He was one of the friendlier weres. "Aye, just knock. He won't mind."

Thoma waved his thanks and walked down the stone paths. They had added some greenery, small shrubs and trees, since his last visit. They had only a handful of one-story houses and a small medical practice. For other services, they used the shops and the harbor in the village.

Children ran past him shrieking, playing a game of tag. Thoma smiled before he stepped onto the front porch of Maxim's house, which was close to the small town center. He knocked.

"Aye." Maxim's deep rumble came through the thick wood, followed by the heavy set of his boots. The door opened. "I've been expecting you." He left the door open and turned back, walking down the hallway. They walked past a living room and what looked like the bedroom into a kitchen.

"Coffee?"

"Yes, please."

Maxim pointed to a chair and turned to the stove, where water was already going. He ground beans in a small electric grinder and then put everything into a coffee press. He got out two mugs, milk, sugar, and the coffee.

"You've come to inquire about the autopsy."

"Naturally," Thoma said with a shrug.

Maxim chuckled. "The old man breathing down your neck?"

"You know how it is."

"Naturally."

Thoma grinned.

Maxim pressed down the sieve of the press and poured the coffee. "Sugar and milk, was it, or...?"

Thoma nodded, and then they sipped their mugs in silence until Thoma had gathered his thoughts. "Do you have anything for me?"

"Nothing we didn't already suspect. Doc is still taking a deeper look, but the head wound is from blunt-force trauma and most probably killed him."

A faint tremor ran through the ground; the island had known, had felt it happening, had felt the rage and the bloodthirst, but having the confirmation was still different.

"The land isn't happy."

"I imagine," Maxim sighed, putting his mug down and looking out the window. "You know why we settled here and built these crumbled ruins from the ground up again?"

Thoma shrugged. He hadn't even been born then, and no one told stories about council decisions. On Thomas's side of the island, only Old Man Nathaniel was still alive from then. Maxim must have been a young wolf at that time, with less gray and fewer lines.

"Because the land welcomed us. We had never been welcomed before. We were a nomadic tribe, wandering from place to place, always to where the opportunity took us. We needed to make money to stay afloat, to feed the young and elderly who couldn't work, to pay for education and medicine and clothing and everything that living costs. Not all the things we did were good and just; we stole, we swindled, we tried to stay alive. And then I came here."

"What brought you here? I can't imagine that you just landed and then easily convinced your other clan members to join you."

Maxim laughed. "It was a job ad. We had split up to find summer work, and I set over. At the very least, I told myself, I could take a few breaths before setting out again. A vacation, you could say. I met your old man."

"Old Man Nathaniel?"

"Your dad."

Thoma furrowed his brows. "No one told me he was part of the council."

"Oh, he was, but years later. When we met in the pub, at that time in the hands of Per's grandfather, he was more suspicious; he kept watching me, just as you're watching me right now." Another chuckle. "I asked what he wanted, and he told me that he'd never seen a dog before. I told him I had never looked a fish in the eye, and here I was doing just that. We fought it out."

"You and my dad got into a fist fight?"

"The old man wasn't too pleased about it."

"That, I can imagine," Thoma muttered into his coffee. He took a sip, closing his eyes in bliss. It tasted heavenly.

"I special order the beans. There are some pleasures in life that should be allowed."

Thoma looked at him, but Maxim's gaze was clear. "What happened after?"

"Hm?"

"The fight."

"Ah. The old man threw us into the cells and told us to cool off. Then your mother came and gave the old man an earful and let us both out. We drank to our new friend-ship. And I returned to the mainland. The job offer was rescinded after the fight."

Thoma tapped his finger on the table.

"Don't be so impatient. A letter arrived almost two years later: a new job offer on the island. I was curious, so I returned and was greeted by your father. He took me to the side and told me they had a lot to do here and that there was an old settlement that could be spruced up if we needed a place to settle and didn't mind the hard work. We didn't, so we spoke to the council, and they voted for us."

"Why?"

Maxim shrugged. "I'm not sure. Some of the magic came with me when I left the island, and the island wanted that bit back, and that was only possible if the clan was with me. It's probably more complicated than that, but that was what your father told me. And so we settled, and you were born, and then..." His eyes went to a faraway place.

"...they died." Thoma finished for him, his heart constricting.

Maxim nodded. "I wish you could have known them later. They were remarkable people. Free and unbound. Not many leave their clan and wander onto the shores of another, even if they have some nebulous familial ties."

"I never found out why they left the north and came here."

Maxim shrugged. "They never told. I'm sure not even the old man knows."

Thoma still wondered. "So what happens now?"

"We will ask questions and try to find that damn pack-age. It wasn't in the shop, so whoever murdered Jonathan may have taken it as well, or someone was in after the murderer and took the opportunity, though that seems unlikely." Maxim stirred his coffee. "Any clue what the package might be?"

Thoma shook his head. "Victor is tight-lipped about it. He says it's a mission, some task he is doing for money. Get the package and deliver it."

"I wonder…" Maxim shook his head. "Doesn't matter." He fixed Thoma with a look. "What do you know about our guest?"

Thoma flushed. Maxim raised an eyebrow. "I… We met a few years ago on the mainland. We…uh…" He waved a hand.

Maxim took pity on him. "I see. And then?"

"We never exchanged numbers and never saw each other again. He was surprised when he met me at the inn."

"You think his surprise was genuine?"

Thoma thought about it. The surprise, the delight, the hesitation, and the sadness, everything had happened so fast that it couldn't have been played, right?

"Nobody is broken."

Those words resonated within him, but had Victor truly meant them as such? They had come together so easily, pleasure given and pleasure received.

"I think so." Thoma swallowed. "Maxim, I…he and I…" Why was this so hard? But he needed to tell Maxim that they had slept together again. "The night Jonathan was murdered, Victor and I shared a bed."

Maxim nodded as if he'd expected as much. "You know when he arrived at the inn that evening?"

Thoma shook his head. "It had been dark and rainy. Thunder and lightning were coming close together." And the music had thundered around him in the same wild rhythm as his heart.

"And during the night? Did you wake up at all? Was he there?"

"I slept through. Per's knocking woke me. I felt him slip out, so then he was at least in bed."

"I'll try to find out when the storm hit us fully to create a timeline. But this means neither of you have an alibi."

Thoma shrugged. "I had no quarrel with Jonathan and no reason to see him dead."

"Everybody says that, and still someone killed him."

A thought came. "Was Jonathan all right?"

Maxim eyed him. "How so?"

"Victor told me that Jonathan was short with him when he asked about the package, and threw him out twice. That didn't sound like the Jonathan I knew." Thoma licked his lips. "Was it because Victor was a stranger?"

Maxim shook his head. "Jonathan had no problems with non-island weres. No, something must have bothered him. I wonder why he didn't come to me."

"Maybe it was nothing."

"Maybe," Maxim said, but he looked troubled.

Victor trekked back to the inn. He scoured the kitchen and found some eggs and bacon in the fridge; that together with a pot of fresh coffee would make up for the lack of anything to eat in the morning and the more than rude awakening.

When he set the small kitchen table for himself, the front door opened and closed. Silence followed, no steps or creaking floorboards—a moment in time, exhaling into the space that was between them. The house shuddered, and Victor shook his head, amused.

Ancestral homes were a special brand of magic. Intelligent people had written papers and books about them, with all kinds of theories, and still no one could really explain them. One side saw them as actual ghosts, floating on another sphere and permeating magic through the thin membrane of the worlds (not that anyone ever could prove that there were other worlds). Others theorized such places formed from magic energy left behind, building up for centuries and generations until it developed a semi-sentient mentality, not really alive nor fully developed, driven by instincts and feelings, bound to the head of the house as if the current owner were an extension of it.

Victor had seen a few ancestral homes, but none had been as strong as this one, almost a living entity.

Footsteps moved closer, and Thoma appeared in the doorway, his eyes cold and distant. He eyed the food. Victor didn't want to invite him, but repudiating Thoma would be like capitulating on their relationship. Even though Victor had let go of the dream of having someone close, maybe they could still be friends.

"Food?"

Thoma was already in the process of shaking his head when his stomach growled. Victor grabbed a second plate while Thoma made himself a cup of coffee. It was a tight fit, and Victor took care to get his limbs out of the way and to not accidentally brush against Thoma. They ate in silence, Thoma's gaze miles away. After they finished, Victor cleared the plates away, and Thoma kept staring into his coffee.

Victor knew where this was going. He leaned back against the counter and crossed his arms. "So, the bad news."

Thoma exhaled. "You don't have an alibi."

"And they think I did it?"

Thoma shrugged. "They'd prefer it."

"And you?"

"It doesn't matter."

"It matters to me." This was important to Victor, more than he'd have thought possible; he wanted Thoma to believe him, to see him as something other than a dumb, violent were.

Thoma exhaled again and curled his shoulders forward. Victor wondered what Thoma was feeling. He could smell anger, arousal, and fear, but no sweat. He wasn't hiding something. So that blend wasn't guilt—more like regret—wariness maybe? Smell worked only with specific emotions. Overpowering the others, they usually created blends, and it wasn't always possible to pinpoint what exactly the person he scented was feeling.

"Don't," Thoma finally said after what felt like hours.

Victor looked away as if slapped. Why was he still doing this to himself?

Because—

He swallowed. That wasn't something he should analyze right now.

"What now?"

Thoma pinched the bridge of his nose. "They're investigating in general, not only you. But you are a suspect. You arrive and someone is dead. This is the first murder in a very long time. Maybe the first ever. So there is that." Mirroring Victor's posture, Thoma leaned back and also crossed his arms. "And why were you sent to get the package? It could have been sent with the postal service. It's suspicious that you came out here specifically to get it and that no one knows what the package is about. No one has come forward claiming to have sent it. Jonathan also has no records of who gave it over." Thoma raised his voice at the end, phrasing it as a question. His gaze was now steady.

Victor looked back over. "It's a *job*."

"What was it you said you do?"

And there it was, the question. Victor didn't like the suspicious glint in those ice-blue eyes. They should ever look only one way at him, focused and with passion and—

He really needed to get his emotions under control.

"This and that; a jack-of-all-trades." It wasn't a lie. He'd done nothing else the last few years. "Trying to stay afloat."

"Which you've always done?" Thoma tried to sound nonchalant.

Victor was done. "If you want to know about me, then ask. Don't do this chicken-shit of an interrogation."

"I'm..."

"Spare me." And with that parting shot, Victor left before he did something he couldn't take back.

THOMA CLOSED HIS eyes and pressed his face into his hands. This was spiraling out of control fast. He looked over at the calendar, the marked-off days creeping closer to a bigger date. The clan was coming ashore in a few days, and then he'd need to deal with all his cousins and elders and their disappointment and tongue clucking, on top of the unhappy island and a murderer on the loose and—

Did it really not matter to him if Victor was the culprit? Was he really that callous? He'd hurt Victor, it was clear in the taut line of Victor's shoulders and the fingers digging into his underarms.

Memories flashed through his mind: "He smells of death"; Jonathan's head caved in; Victor's intense gaze.

Victor was big and powerful, his hands could crush bones, and yet he'd been so gentle with Thoma, careful and honest.

Thoma shivered as the memory of those fingers drifted over his skin. He'd been almost everything Thoma had ever wanted. Victor had been open with him, showing him what he enjoyed and never too afraid to ask for it, and Thoma...

He rose from the chair, feeling cramped and stiff, and dialed the number of the pub to order dinner for the next few days and arrange the feast for his clan. Clair said she would tell Per and asked him if he was all right. He grunted something affirmative and cut the call amidst her protests, wincing already at the earful she would give him later. Later. Everything else could come later. When Thoma was less different, less out of it, less fragile.

But hadn't he been fragile now for three years? When would it finally stop? He was sick of being a shadow of himself, a shadow of what he'd once been, shunned by the others, unable to do what he wanted. But wasn't he also doing what he loved?

Thoma's eyes fell back to the date. The day the selkies would come was the same day the ferry would return. Victor would leave, and Thoma would be too busy to take note of it.

He walked up the stairs, stopping on the landing leading up to the first floor. The house was silent. Nothing moved, neither a wolf nor the ghosts. Had Victor left?

He stepped forward, stopping in front of the door, knocking before he could catch himself. "Victor, you in?" He'd no clue what he would say if Victor answered, but there was only more silence. Something moved in the shadows. Anticipation? Thoma pressed the handle down, praying it was locked, but it opened under his hands.

The room was unoccupied.

Thoma released a breath he'd involuntarily been holding and slipped in. The room was neat, neater than Thomas had ever seen. As if Victor hadn't occupied the space at all. The wolves at the pub were always rowdy and messy; Clair had complained about them often. Not many of them visited the bookstore, but when they did, they never kept to the organizational systems, and more than one book had come back creased and dirty with only an apologetic shrug as explanation. Even Maxim, who had some standards, kept his office in chaotic clutter, with papers and books stacked in precarious towers and old coffee cups collecting mold.

On the washbasin was a single toothbrush lying parallel to a razor and a tube of toothpaste. A towel was draped in straight lines across the chair by the table. On the table lay a notebook with a pen next it, each placed in perfect parallel lines. The suitcase was open next to the table, clothing neatly folded and stacked. The bed was made, the corners tucked in with ninety-degree angles.

Thoma walked to the suitcase and picked through it as carefully as possible. Everything seemed to be in order. He pulled out a small leather case with some documents; all were addressed to the name Victor had given him on the check-in paper.

He put everything back.

He checked under the bed, the small dresser, and the nightstand. There was no package to be found. Thoma even opened the windows and looked around the roof. Nothing hidden out there.

He knocked on the walls and the furniture, knowing there couldn't be a false bottom, but paranoia compelled him to. The house answered with a titter, giving an almost ticklish shudder.

Straightening up, Thoma felt foolish. If Victor had the package, would he leave it here?

Another shudder went through the house, giving Thoma a warning. He looked around, but nothing seemed out of place. He slipped out, closed the door, and tiptoed to his own door just as steps came up. He held his breath and waited until Victor had slipped through his door, closing it behind him; only then did Thoma exhaled and walk through his own. There he waited, his back pressed against the wood, counting his heartbeats. When no sound came, no Victor running up and demanding what he'd been doing in his room, he allowed himself to relax.

What should he do now?

CHAPTER 5

SOMEONE HAD BEEN in his room. Victor knew the moment he stepped in. He'd taken a long walk down the meadows to calm himself down; Thoma had rattled him badly. He had told himself to give up, and yet he couldn't stop the hope, couldn't stop that strange feeling in his chest that expanded every time he looked at Thoma. And while he'd been out, someone had taken the opportunity to take a closer look through his belongings.

Victor looked around. Nothing was missing and everything was in order, and yet someone had riffled through his things.

Only one person could have done it.

Victor sank down on the bed, feeling unmoored.

Maybe he should've stayed in the military. While it hadn't been easy, it'd been less complicated, at least on the surface, and everything else could be ignored. Now, every step he took, every turn he made, he ran into some complex pattern of life, and he didn't know how to handle it anymore.

Victor told himself that it would be only for a few more days, and even if he got charged with the murder, he might be able to slip away, the mission be damned. If Stephen needed the package so badly, he could come and deal himself with this insane place.

His fingers skittered over his thighs, his mind rest-less. He wouldn't be able to settle down. He grabbed his notebook and went downstairs, through the living room, to the wooden terrace. The water level had risen, almost lapping over the planks. Victor watched the small waves, but the sun was hot and, after the walk, he could use some cooling down. He took off his shoes and socks, rolled up his pant legs, and sat down, letting his feet dangle in the cool water.

Then he opened the notebook, squinted into the sea, and started to draw. He'd taken art up as a way to pass the time in the odd hours he'd been on call, on the nights he couldn't sleep, or whenever he needed a break from everything else. The hobby had persisted into his civil-ian life, not that he was any good at it. But it calmed him down and gave his fingers something to do while his mind sorted through everything that had been happening.

The sun had risen high when he put the book to the side and lay back, letting the sun warm him. Like most weres, he liked to curl up in a sunny spot and soak the heat in, let the cozy warm lull him into a drowsy sleep. The water was a pleasant counterpoint, the cry of the seagulls only a minor disturbance.

It was peaceful—

A sharp pull, and he was spluttering in the water. It went up his mouth and nose, filling his lungs. He tried to kick after what had grabbed him, but it held fast. He lost his orientation, panic gripping him, squeezing rational thought out of him. He swallowed more water, the salti-ness making him nearly vomit… He was…was…

…dark water closing in, the fiery red shine of the boat disrupted by the waves, dead men sinking beside him, the sound of explosions muffled beyond recognition…sinking deeper and deeper.

Death was grasping for him.

It was calm under the waves.

Suddenly, he was moved up and up, back into the light, his body on something hard; he heaved and vomited, crawling forward, hands helping him get farther. The sun was hot above him. He shivered, his mind detangling from the memories of the mission that had ended with a sunken boat and half of his team dead.

Stephen had saved his life that day, for the first time.

When he finally was able to breathe and think again, he rolled onto his back, looking up into Thoma's worried face. Thoma's hair was plastered against his forehead, water running down and dropping onto the wooden terrace.

"What happened?" Victor rolled onto his side as a sudden coughing fit overcame him, and he vomited more water. When he was done, he looked at Thoma, who worried his lip between his teeth.

"My cousins' take on a joke."

"A joke? I could've died." Victor sat up, cross-legged, looking pointedly at Thoma.

Thoma snorted. "The water here isn't deep enough for that."

Victor looked back to the water lapping at the terrace structure; even from here, he could make out the bottom. Embarrassed, he scratched at his neck. "They surprised me."

"If you say so."

Then it hit him. Cousins. And there he saw them, sleek seal bodies disappearing into deeper waters. Victor crossed his arms. He'd heard of creatures like this but had never encountered one before. Different lands had different stories, different names, different types—but always reclusive. He tried to find the correct term for those he saw here. "They are selkies." He watched Thoma. Guilt etched around his eyes, a slight tightening of his mouth, a flash in the blue eyes. "And you are one too."

"And what if I am?" Thoma raised his chin.

Victor shook his head. "The seals kept watching me. I should've guessed." Cold wind blew in from the sea. Thoma shivered. "You're cold."

"Duh." Thoma rolled his eyes and hugged himself.

Victor grinned, and they looked at each other, and everything was washed away, and Victor discarded all the alarms in his head screaming that this was a bad idea. He moved on instinct.

Victor was kissing him. Again. Nice and soft, lips on lips, not coaxing, not demanding or making impossible promises. Thoma swayed back. Victor watched him with dark eyes, unfathomable and opaque.

"You should rinse your mouth."

Victor blinked and then he bowed forward, hands on his knees, and laughed, on the verge of being hysterical. Then he stopped and shot Thoma such a quicksilver grin that Thoma wondered why he hadn't fallen in love earlier. Or maybe he had.

In this moment, with that grin, carefree and open, Victor was everything.

Victor sprang up and grabbed the teacup Thoma had left there when he'd come to Victor's rescue. He took a gulp, grimaced, and rinsed his mouth, spitting the rest into the ocean. Thoma was sure this was meant as a rude gesture. Then Victor looked at him, looked at him as if he was the entire world, everything Victor ever wanted, and Thoma broke open. He stood and grabbed Victor's face and kissed him and kissed him—never wanted to stop kissing him. Everything narrowed down to Victor: his smell, the texture of his skin, the taste of his mouth, his fingers reaching every patch of Thoma's skin. He didn't even realize they had relocated until Victor lowered him gently onto the bed, spreading him out like a pliable puppet. Thoma should be embarrassed at being seen like this—too far gone to protest, to hide, to run. But Victor didn't say anything. He took his time, nipping and tasting, stroking over quivering thighs and legs, drinking moans from Thoma's mouth, coaxing everything that he was from out of him, all the desires and feelings he'd kept tightly locked away.

Thoma let himself be carried higher and higher to a blinding crescendo, and for a second, everything halted— the house shivering, the ghosts whispering, the magic of the land curling lazily—before it came crashing down.

When he could focus again, Thoma found Victor on his side, facing him, his fingers tracing an idle pattern into Thoma's skin. So much lay in Victor's eyes. Thoma knew, without a doubt, that if he wanted, he could claim this man or let himself be claimed.

But how would that work? Thoma here and Victor not? The wolf wouldn't bind himself to the island. There was a restlessness in his gaze; he was not a man who'd settle down. And Thoma didn't want to bind himself to an impossible dream.

"For as long as you stay."

Victor closed his eyes. He didn't quite relax, but he exhaled. "Okay." And then he rolled on top of Thoma, kissing him languidly, not to arouse, but to give, to reassure.

When they broke for breath, Victor's eyes were still unreadable, almost pensive. Thoma reached out and traced the bridge of his nose, then down to the lips.

Victor pressed a kiss against his fingers.

"Let me show you the island."

Victor smiled. "I'd like that."

THEY SHOWERED AND went to their respective rooms to put on the appropriate clothing. Victor looked at the rumpled bed and wondered. Thoma had done such a turnaround that it had almost given Victor whiplash. He'd been prepared for another rebuttal, but Thoma had accepted him. He considered the shift of heart for a moment, then decided to go with it.

Two days. He'd only two days left. Maybe three, depending on when the ferry arrived.

The fallout would hurt. Thoma had made it clear that they would only have this time, until Victor left, and they both knew that Victor would leave. This island wasn't his land. The weres had been accepted by the magic, but he— No, it didn't want him here. The land buzzed under his feet.

The weather outside was beautiful. Thoma grabbed Victor's hand and entwined their fingers. They smiled at each other.

Victor could handle heartache. He was a big boy. He hadn't allowed himself to give what was growing between them a name, hadn't been ready to give it a face and therefore power.

The moment he left, when everything was said and done, then he would dare to name it, to exorcize it.

Unperturbed by and unaware of Victor's inner turmoil, Thoma dragged him out, passing grazing sheep who watched them with dark, beady eyes, through underbrush and over creeks, back to the grove Victor had seen the other day. They didn't stop at the clearing Victor had found; instead, Thoma led him deeper, until they were in a small meadow, with dancing butterflies and soft, bowing windflowers.

"This is my secret spot." Thoma spun around, his arms spread wide. "Okay, the island is small, and it's probably the secret spot of a lot of people. But we don't talk about it."

"It's beautiful."

Then Thoma grabbed his hand again and dragged him farther, a small path suddenly revealed before them, leading through hills until they stood atop the cliff. The wind was stronger here, dancing around their clothes, grabbing for their hair. Thoma smiled, free and unguarded, and Victor greedily drank Thoma's pleasure in, cataloging every shift in Thoma's face, taking mental picture after mental picture.

"This is the ocean." Thoma stretched his arms wide, as if he wanted to gather the sea and press it close. "And this"—he turned to the island—"is Seagull Island, home to four selkie families and one werewolf tribe. A few more folks have come, intending to travel through, and never left. Some have mixed blood, but that doesn't matter."

Victor stepped closer, taking Thoma in his arms. Exhilarated by the feeling that he was, for the moment, allowed to do so. "The island is full of old magic," Thoma explained, leaning against Victor. "We don't know what happened here. Some say a mage built a barrier around it to hide. Others argue that the number of magical folks who have lived here have drenched the land over the centuries. That it has developed a mind of its own—not sentient, but aware." He shrugged. Victor felt the movement against his skin; he nuzzled into Thoma's soft neck.

"Currently..." His breath hitched, and Victor smiled. Thoma swatted him. "Currently it's unhappy. Blood was spilled, and someone needs to pay a price before the land can settle down again."

Victor felt the faint tremor under his feet, the unhappy hum. "What can I do?"

"Nothing."

Victor felt Thoma's heartbeat against his own, calm and reassuring. "And if I'm the killer?"

A seagull made a lazy circle above them. If Victor didn't know better, he'd think a selkie was keeping an eye on him.

"Maybe you did. Maybe you didn't. I don't know you. For all I know, you could be a bloodthirsty serial killer, and yet...and yet..."

He didn't finish, and Victor hugged him tighter. Technically he was a bloodthirsty serial killer, but being paid by the government made all the difference, law-wise.

"Clair tells me I should listen more to my instincts, and this is me doing that."

Victor moved them a bit apart so that he could look at Thoma. His expression was confused, but there was a resolute line around his mouth, and lips begging to be kissed.

Victor obliged.

The wind still tried to tear them apart, the island rumbled under their feet, and the sun burned on his neck, but Victor had never felt this good.

When they broke apart, Thoma looked dazed. "I think...I think we should go back."

"Oh." Victor raised an eyebrow, and Thoma swatted him again.

"Food. Clair will be around with it soon."

"No pub?"

"I don't think either of us want to face the stares."

Victor nodded.

Thoma led them back toward the inn, and as Victor followed, he couldn't help thinking.

Maybe...just maybe...

WHEN THEY EMERGED from the woods, their hands clasped, Thoma saw that Clair was almost to the inn. She turned when she heard their steps. First she furrowed her brows, then she looked pointedly at their entwined hands and at Thoma. He blushed, refusing to move his hand away.

After they had brought the food inside, Clair studied him closer. People said that, due to her heritage, she saw more than a normal mortal would, but she'd never denied nor confirmed those rumors.

Thoma could see that she wanted to ask questions, but he only shrugged at her, and she shook her head, amused, then pecked him on the cheek and flitted away.

Thoma turned to Victor and caught the tail-end of an emotion crossing his face. It was intense and fierce, and it shivered down Thoma's spine. He needed to swallow before he could speak; Victor traced the movement with his eyes.

"Bad dog," Thoma hissed without heat.

Victor threw his head back and laughed. Even knowing there was no future for them didn't lessen the illusion they had created. For the moment, they could pretend, and then return to how they'd been before, two ships in the night, passing each other.

Thoma gestured to the table, where a mouthwatering feast was waiting. Pot roast and creamy mashed potatoes, green beans with bacon, and Per's famous apple pie. Clair had included two bottles of the cider Victor seemed to love, and he made grabby hands for one of those.

"Best cider I've ever tasted. There's nothing that compares on the mainland."

"What is out there?" Thoma asked curiously. He'd only been to the city a few times, and only to the city. Every place else, he'd only read about.

Victor cut his share of pot roast into precise pieces, chewed one, and swallowed. "Everything." He took a sip of the cider. "Mountains that were moved by giants. The trench where the witches' fists crashed down when they rebelled against the fifth witch king. The desert of tears, where the sound of weeping grows stronger the closer to death you are." He looked at his food. "The splintered moon and the lost stars."

"And you have seen all that?"

"Well, the moon is right out there." Amused, Victor pointed a finger toward the window. "I've seen impossible things happen. I was out there when the stars went missing. I..." His fingers skittered over the table. "I've done a lot of things I'm not proud of. Death follows me like an old companion. I know others can smell it on me."

Thoma put his fork down. He pressed his many questions down and settled on: "What did you do?"

"I hunted monsters."

Thoma sucked in his breath, but before he could comment, or accuse, or whatever this was coursing through his body, somebody pounded against the door.

He scrunched his brows, but the pounding didn't stop. He shoved to his feet and went down the hallway, Victor behind him.

Thoma threw the door open.

Maxim watched him wearily, and the two wolves behind him looked grim.

"We're here to search Victor's room." His eyes flicked to a point above Thoma's shoulder.

"Why?" Thoma wanted to say that he'd already done that, but with Victor lurking at his back, that wasn't an admission he was prepared to make.

"We got a tip." Maxim looked troubled.

"No," Thoma said as Victor said, "All right."

Thoma turned his head and stared at Victor, who threw him an easy smile.

"I've nothing to hide."

VICTOR STEPPED BACK, and Thoma made room to let the wolves in. They walked up the stairs, Victor following them. The door was not locked, so Maxim and his two deputies spilled in while Thoma took a few steps into the room and Victor leaned against the frame.

They worked methodically. Maxim went through the suitcase, sifting through the clothes and checking the contents of the leather case. He lingered there for a moment and then moved on. He was about to move to the dresser when Sal gave a shout from where he was half crouched under the bed. Then he dragged out a small package.

Thoma had trouble understanding what he saw.

Victor went stiff.

The package was small and wrinkled, wrapped in brown paper. It had a few dark spots on the side.

Maxim took it carefully from Sal and sniffed. "Blood." Big bold letters on the outside spelled Victor's name.

There had been nothing under the bed when Victor had gone out, and since then, he'd been with Thoma. Had he brought it back when he'd gone out? Had he slipped out in the night? As he could have the night when Jonathan had been killed?

But Victor stared at the package as if seeing it for the first time. There was confusion, then his eyes flicked to Thoma, and his expression changed. Something rippled there, devastating and soul-crushing. He opened his mouth but closed it again. His body seemed to slump, crumpling into himself like a puppet with its strings cut.

Victor's gaze looked so far away.

Maxim sighed, then he turned to Victor. "Captain Victor Lucien, you're under arrest on the suspicion of having committed the murder of Jonathan Bellwood."

For a long moment, it was unclear if Victor had even heard him, then he nodded slowly. "Aye."

He let himself be led out, no fight, no argument, and no gaze back to Thoma.

Everything inside Thoma hurt.

CHAPTER 6

THEY WALKED IN silence. The path curved back toward the city, which surprised Victor. He'd thought he would be marched to the were settlement and prosecuted on the spot.

They walked down to the harbor through a back alley with few people. At the harbor, they turned right toward an old brick building, its façade weathered and stained, its windows covered by metal gratings.

They piled in. The air was musty and stale. They led Victor through a spacious room. A pile of junk was stacked to one side, and the rest of the room held a few desks, most of which were coated with a layer of dust. The building had an atmosphere of disuse.

They stepped through a door to the right and went down a small flight of stairs.

Rows of metal bars and stone walls greeted them.

"This is the old police building. It's mostly used for storage now," Maxim said when Victor threw him a questioning gaze. "It has temporary holding cells. Long-term prisoners are shipped to the mainland."

Victor nodded and eyed the holding cell with trepidation. No were liked to be caged—no one liked to be caged.

Maxim opened a cell door, and Victor walked in. It was spacious enough. A small bench was pushed against the back wall; it would be very uncomfortable to sleep on. There was a toilet behind a flimsy screen, and a sink. Lovely.

The steel was reinforced. Were-proof. Even lovelier.

"Sal, go check for some blankets."

The wolf on the right nodded and left. The other studied them and apparently decided that Victor was no threat; they followed Sal out.

Maxim stood before the cell, the package still in one hand, watching him thoughtfully. As if Victor was a puzzle for which Maxim didn't know what the picture was supposed to look like.

Victor sat down on the bench and said, "You're wishing I did it."

"In my position, Captain Lucien, wouldn't you hope as well that the stranger in town did it?"

"Ex-captain."

Maxim moved his hands and the package behind his back. "What did you do?"

"I hunted." Victor grinned broadly, showing the rows of his teeth.

Maxim hummed, not rising to the bait. "I heard about your kind. Monsters going after monsters. Special-ops teams that are dispatched to rein in the unruly and dangerous."

"That way no one could call me a murderer."

"If that makes it easier for you to bear."

"We all have our reasons." Victor let his arms rest on his thighs.

"Isn't that the excuse for everything?"

Victor answered with a shrug. "Probably."

Maxim chuckled, and Sal returned with his arms filled with dusty blankets and two limp cushions. "This was all I could find." He almost sounded apologetic.

Maxim opened the door, and Victor stayed back on the bench to make it easier on everyone.

"Chief, we need to go." The other stood in the door, his eyes on a wristwatch.

"Aye."

Sal finished and walked out.

Maxim left the cell, locked the door behind himself, and turned to walk away.

"What is in the package?"

Maxim looked back over his shoulder, then down to the package in his hands. He was studying it as if he'd forgotten that it was still there. "I see," was all he said, then he walked out

The heavy door to the holding-cell-lined hall fell closed. Victor could barely make out the sound of the turn of the key.

Then there was only silence.

He got up and tried the bars and the door, but they didn't budge. And if they had, would breaking himself out make any sense? There was no way off the island for at least two more days, and even then, he doubted the sea captain would take him, and even if he would, the islanders would search the ferry up and down.

No.

Victor shook his head to clear it and sat back down on the bench. The blankets didn't cushion anything, and the bench was way too small for his frame. Now came the hard part—being bored. He'd had long stretches of boredom when he'd served. Times, sometimes days, when they sat around and did nothing, waiting for a call for action to come through. But then there had been distraction, even if what was at hand had been slight: a bit of drabbling, some reading, and some fucking.

He could fuck himself here, but having only the bars delineating his area of such a large, exposed room was a massive turn-off.

Where had the package come from?

Would Thoma really frame him like that? He'd been in the room while Victor had been out, Victor had smelled him, but would he really do that? What would be his gain? Or had Thoma tried to distract him? Distract from the fact that Thoma himself had killed Jonathan...but no one had even considered that possibility. They had been focused on Victor. Would Maxim ignore leads like that?

Any answer to these questions was possible. Victor didn't really know any of these people.

He'd met Thoma in a gallery. Victor had only gone because a friend begged him to attend so that it wouldn't be empty there. Everything had been boring: the people, the venue, the food, and the pictures—clashes of color that were supposedly a commentary on society; only people with an art degree could have comprehended them.

Amid the ebb and flow of high-pitched laughter and the droning of pretentious words had stood Thoma, his eyes fixed on a picture of blue and turquoise with dots of white. Victor had thought it showed the ocean and its treacherous plains, but it was titled "Vomit No.2." And yet Thoma had stared for so long that Victor felt compelled to walk over and talk to him about it. From there, their conversation had transitioned to the ocean and the sea and the world beyond, and then they had walked out and gotten something to eat and talked more. And when Victor had asked Thoma to his hotel room, Thoma hadn't hesitated.

Victor sighed. Light filtered through a narrow window, giving him a track of the time. It went slowly.

After that night, Thoma had vanished, and now they had met three years later, both changed. Victor had searched for Thoma, had even asked his pals and the gallery owner if they knew each other, but no one remembered Thoma, as if he'd been a ghost granted one night of manifestation to visit the earthly planes.

Stranger things had happened in this world.

Yet Victor hadn't been able to put Thoma to rest; his mind always looped back to the man standing lost and forlorn in front of the giant painting.

And then, when Victor had almost given up, Thoma was in front of him once more, had allowed Victor to hold him close, again and again...so why should he want to harm Victor?

Maybe to get him off the island. But it'd been clear that Victor would be leaving, that their days were numbered. And even if that were the reason, why murder young Jonathan over it? Did Jonathan's murder have a motive? Did it need one? In Victor's experience, motives were a media construct to ensure that death made sense to the viewer and reader. Real life seldom needed a motive. People killed other people because they wanted to and because they could, because they had the opportunity. Nothing more was needed.

Victor scrubbed his hands over his face and exhaled.

In the end, whatever he wanted didn't matter. Only facts remained. Victor hadn't killed the man, and he hadn't taken the package. Thoma had been in his room, and shortly after, the package had been found there. When had Victor last looked under the bed?

Ridiculous.

Noise caught Victor's attention: steps coming closer, followed by the scrap of the key in the keyhole, the handle pressing down. Victor stayed seated, trying to appear non-threatening. The door swung open, and Maxim looked at him. Not quite smiling but more relaxed. That must be a good sign, right?

"Victor, I just heard..." And then he stumbled, crashing down on the floor, knocking his head hard. He groaned and then went still.

Victor looked toward the door. Had the shadows moved? Maxim hadn't bothered to turn on the lights. Victor squinted, but they didn't move again, and Maxim was more important.

He scrambled forward, pressing against the bars.

"Maxim?" he called. "Wake up!"

This was bad. They couldn't put this on him, but they might try anyway. "Somebody! Help! Hello? Someone up there?"

Victor shouted and shouted, his voice almost giving out, until steps pounded over the floor, quickly drawing closer.

Thoma came to a skittering stop in the open doorway, his mouth open, and then his eyes found Maxim's crumpled figure. "What...?" He was moving, crouching and checking Maxim over. "He is alive. I need to get..." His eyes met Victors, then he shook himself and was gone again.

Victor slumped and exhaled, ready for all of this to be finally over.

THOMA WATCHED AS they heaved the stretcher up and carefully moved Maxim out of the room. Doc had assured them that, while Maxim had taken quite the blow, with that thick skull he should survive. The doctor would keep an eye on him; all anyone else could do was wait for him to wake up.

Trevor watched on with cold eyes that blazed when he looked toward Victor. He was already opening his mouth when Sal put a hand on his shoulder, shaking his head.

There was no way Victor could have had anything to do with it. A witch could have put up a spell, but wolves didn't have that kind of magic, even crossbreeds.

Still, this was bad.

Thoma had finally found the courage to phone Maxim and tell him that he'd snooped in Victor's room and that there hadn't been any package whatsoever there when he'd done so. There was no sense in Victor killing Jonathan. At the worst, the office would have opened today and Victor could have gotten the package. And there was no indication that Victor had ever been to the island or had known Jonathan in the past.

Thoma shook himself and looked over to Victor; the others had filtered out as if they had forgotten that Thoma had come with them.

"Did you do it?" Victor's gaze was steady and closed off. His arms were crossed.

"Did I do what?" He hadn't killed Jonathan or attacked Maxim, if that is what Victor was asking. But he couldn't be, could he?

"Did you put the package under my bed?"

That stopped Thoma. Why would he—? Oh... "You smelled me."

Victor's grin was full of teeth. Then his posture deflated and he rested his arms on his thighs. "Why?"

Thoma shrugged. He hadn't been sure himself, at that time, what had driven him. "Curiosity, mostly."

"Mostly."

Thoma sighed and looked away. "I wanted to make sure

that you didn't have the package, that you hadn't killed Jonathan. That I—" He licked his lips and fell silent. *That I hadn't fallen in love with a murderer.* A too-heavy thought, better left alone. He pushed it away.

"I told you, I hunted monsters. I killed. I have blood on my hands, even some innocent." Victor could have been speaking of the weather, his voice was neutral, almost matter-of-fact.

But why was Victor telling him that now? After... "Not finding it made it more likely that you weren't involved."

"You believe that."

"I don't know what I should believe. Everything has gone sideways since you arrived, and I don't know what I should do."

"Thoma."

"I just—fuck—I don't know." Thoma snorted. "Once, my path was clear. I knew where I should put my feet to start and every following step. Then the path vanished, and I found a new one, and then you arrived and everything went to shit again, and I can't deal with that again..."

"There is nothing to deal with."

Thoma whipped his head around.

Victor stared at him grimly, his jaw tight but his brow smooth.

"I'm here now, and soon I'll be gone. The ferry will come and take me away."

Thoma swallowed. "Yes, I know, and yet..." His mind was jumbled, his heartbeat heavy, drowning in his ears. The words on his tongue didn't make much sense to him. "I wanted..." What did he really want? Something for himself? Something only he could have? To be selfish for once? It felt as if he was asking for something forbidden, something that by law and nature shouldn't be his. And yet, hadn't he given enough? Hadn't he adhered to his duty with all he'd had left? Wasn't his punishment over?

"I know." Victor's eyes almost glowed in the shadows.

"You know?" Thoma crossed his arms and stared at Victor incredulously. "You know what it feels like to have nothing to yourself, as if you're fighting against a current that is endless and all-encompassing, hell-bent on drowning you?"

Victor watched him. "I fought in wars, against mercenaries, against bandits. I killed and injured people, good people, even innocent people. I killed the last dragon. I hunted down fairies. I laid traps for mountain trolls. I went where they pointed me to go, to rein in those who'd gone out of control, who'd endangered the others. Government-funded monster hunters. I lost who I had been. I was always on the move, always waiting for the next mission, the next target. Drowning? I'm not sure when I last saw the water's surface."

"I'm sorry."

But Victor shook his head. "No, I'm sorry. I shouldn't've said that. Your pain is your own."

"I—"

Shouting from the other room made Thoma lose his thoughts. Fast steps sounded, and then Trevor entered the room, triumphantly holding up the tatters of the packing paper. Thoma stared at it, his thoughts at odds with what he saw.

He stood before Trevor in a flash, his hands stretching already for it.

Trevor pulled it out of reach, but Thoma would have none of that. "Show me. Now."

The magic of the land obeyed. A tremor rumbled under their feet, like the flick of a finger, barely there, but Trevor gulped and handed the package and its contents over.

Thoma freed the object of the cocoon of remaining wrapping, blinking at it. Fabric, flowing and rippling like water. Thoma gulped. "This is…"

"Yes," Trevor hissed. His body was strung tight beside Thoma, his face full of glee.

This changed things, tremendously, irreversibly.

Thoma turned to Victor, whose burning gaze was fixed on the fabric. He stood proud, a perfect soldier, his hands behind his back. Waiting…he was waiting to be judged, expecting to be found guilty of whatever crime the contents of the package implied, Thoma realized.

"It's a selkie coat." Thoma's voice was hoarse, almost a whisper, but perfectly clear in the small room. Trevor bounced on his feet.

"Oh." That was all Victor said. Because he must know what this meant. Someone had stolen a selkie skin, had made a selkie suffer. The selkies would want justice. Anyone trading selkie skins was put to death.

"Give the skin back. It's evidence." Trevor stretched his hand for it, a greedy gleam in his eyes.

Thoma sidestepped him.

Trevor furrowed his brows and followed, crowding Thoma against the doorframe. Over his shoulder, Thoma saw Victor get closer to the bars.

"I said, it is mine," Trevor growled close to his face.

"This is a selkie's. Remember the rules of the land." Thoma dove out from under Trevor, then folded the skin up quickly.

Sal stepped through the door as Trevor made another grab for the skin. He watched the scene with a raised eyebrow, then stepped between them, handing a small bag to Thoma.

Trevor glowered at Sal, but Thoma smiled gratefully. "They will be here tomorrow. I'll present the case then."

"You hope they will spare him." Sal's voice was smooth.

"It's a misunderstanding."

Trevor snorted. "You really believe that. They'll never believe you, but do what you want," he spat, and with a last malicious glance at Victor, he stalked out, almost shoving Sal out of the way.

Sal shook his head and followed.

"Thoma."

But Thoma shook his head, the bag pressed close to his chest. Having a skin in his hands felt cruel and bittersweet, and Thoma had no clue what to do with the emotions churning through him. "I need to think."

He stepped through the door and locked it behind him.

Victor didn't call again.

Thoma sat on his bed, staring at the package resting in his lap. Going over events again and again. The hardening of Victor's jaw, the flash of something—pain, desperation, guilt?—in his eyes. Trevor's greedy fingers stretching for the package. Thoma's own feelings when he touched the skin.

A selkie skin.

Thoma stretched his trembling fingers out, resting his fingertips lightly on it. Felt the sensation of it having been ripped away from him. He'd trusted that friend, the one who had taken it from him and burned it by accident.

His cousins had drowned that friend in the sea, not because they felt sorry for Thoma but because they could and no one had held them back. They had made their contempt clear. Thoma had been at fault for being too trusting, being too caught up in the matters of the land dwellers. He'd thought himself better than his brethren.

And they had been right. It was Thoma's responsibility to shoulder.

And Thoma had done so, for the last three years.

He wondered about the unfortunate selkie who had lost their skin. Hopefully they were still alive and Thoma could give it back. Many selkies lost their minds in search of their taken skin, never stopping, always hoping, slowly descending into madness.

Thoma had been "lucky" that his skin had burned away before his eyes. A search would've been fruitless.

Everything in him wanted to possess the skin: claim it and make it his own. But that was impossible. One selkie, one skin. No more, no less.

He put the package to the side and lay down flat.

Would he be able to persuade Old Man Nathaniel? That someone had sent Victor, that he hadn't even touched the package, hadn't known what was in it? Victor had come for the skin, yes, but he hadn't known.

Thoma groaned. This would never save him.

No, he needed to stay positive, think positive, believe that there was a solution, a way out. Otherwise...otherwise, he'd lose everything, again, and be stuck on this cursed island forever.

It was early morning when they came. Victor had lain down beside the bench with the blankets and cushion arranged nestlike. Victor hadn't needed a nest for a long time, not since he'd been a lad. Seeking comfort had been burned out of him in the military—not that one didn't need it, but seeking it was fruitless.

He'd lain down amidst the dusty smell of mothballs and something slightly moldy, and waited.

When the sun came up, steps came closer. Somber steps, Victor thought, if the mood of steps could be established based on how they sounded.

Those who stepped into the hall through the doorway weren't weres. They had ice-blue eyes like Thoma, but with a cold sheen to them, as if Victor were staring into the waters of the unrelenting sea. They were led by the man who had sat next to Victor, what felt like years ago.

The selkies had come for him.

Faster than Victor had anticipated, but then, the earlier they got it over with, the better.

The old man opened the cell door and stepped to the side. The others waited. Victor carefully looked from face to face trying to find Thoma, but he was, mercifully, not with the entourage. Victor slumped with relief and stood up. They apparently expected that he would come of his own free will, yet when he stepped forward a ripple went through the group, like a wave on a windy day. Only the old man didn't show his nerves.

He hoped Thoma wouldn't come. Wouldn't witness whatever happened next.

Victor had felt the faint drumming of it in the night and cursed: a mate bond had formed between him and Thoma, early, faint, fragile, but there. Neither of them had committed to it yet. With a little time and rest, Thoma would be as right as rain.

Victor walked out of the cell, his back straight, his head high.

The old man nodded at him.

The selkies parted before him, their eyes still cold and far away. As if they didn't care—he was only someone they needed to judge, and then they would go on with their lives. He was nothing to them.

Victor walked through the crowd to the old office, then out the door. He blinked into the rising sun. Fog hung low over the sea and the town, as if this was some gothic novel and monsters would soon emerge from the hazy white.

Victor almost snorted; the monsters had arrived long ago.

The old man stepped up to him and pointed down a path to the right. Victor nodded and set foot on it. The selkie rearguard remained somber and silent. There was no one outside yet, so no one could interfere or gawk at them. That suited Victor. He'd always shouldered the consequences of his actions, and this time would be no different.

A selkie skin.

He wondered if Stephen knew what the package had contained.

The path wound along the cliffs, veering sharply right before the were village and leading up a knoll. A ring of selkies already waited there. The hill had a small plateau on top; it looked manmade, or at least as though it had been enhanced by those who lived here. There was no grass, only dirt and a few benches. In the middle was an old fire pit, blackened by many uses. Next to it waited two huge people. Not the biggest creatures Victor had ever seen, but the biggest in human form. He swallowed as he saw the two gigantic axes they held.

Victor had a very clear idea how this would play out.

The circle opened for him, and two selkies put their hands on Victor's shoulders and guided him forward.

Closer to the middle and the axes. The subtle pressure indicated that he was to drop to his knees. He went carefully, sitting down on his heels, his palms on his thighs facing up.

Old Man Nathaniel stepped in front of him.

"Victor Lucien—"

"Stop!"

Victor closed his eyes in despair when he recognized Thoma's voice. He turned his head slowly, and the axemen shifted as well. A group of weres had arrived, crowding behind the selkies, led by Trevor, who watched Victor with a satisfied tilt to his head. There was no evidence that Trevor had caused this situation, but increasingly, Victor had his suspicions.

It didn't matter. There was nothing Victor could prove.

Thoma stumbled up the hill, the selkies parting and then closing ranks again, and nearly toppled the old man over.

Chapter 7

Thoma came to a sliding stop between Old Man Nathaniel and Victor.

"Thoma."

"He is innocent." Thoma exhaled. "I wanted to talk to you before going to the police station, but you'd already taken him."

"Someone informed us about what happened." Old Man Nathaniel's eyes flickered over the gathered, his gaze resting for a moment on Trevor.

Thoma snarled. What the old man implied was clear: Thoma hadn't informed him, the clan head—instead, an outsider had done so.

Those nearly translucent eyes skipped back to Thoma, studying him. "Aren't you letting your emotions rule?"

"It's not possible."

Thoma's cousins tittered and giggled.

"I can't form bonds anymore." Admitting it hurt. Selkies bonded, forming connections to other selkies when they did. His mother had once explained to him that there were imprints of each other's emotions, their feelings, like a warm pulse next to one's own. At least that's how it should have been...and how it was.

Because Thoma was lying. He'd formed a bond, years ago, in a single night. Since then, he'd fought it with everything he was, had let other emotions take front-row seats: guilt, anger, hate. But the bond had been there, waiting, a part of him. It had never gone away, even when his skin was torn from him.

Because magic was powered by will and intention. A selkie's magic wasn't situated in their skin; he should have understood that when he'd been able to see the ancestor ghosts and the magic of the island. He wasn't sure what he was anymore, but he hadn't lost everything.

The thought surprised him.

He hadn't lost it all.

Thoma swallowed.

"I see," Old Man Nathaniel said slowly.

"Victor and Thoma swimming under the sea, K-I-S-S-I-N-G," his cousins sang.

The old man threw them a gaze, which stopped them, but their smiles stayed malicious and the tittering in their back ranks didn't stop.

"It doesn't matter. There will be justice for the skin and the wolves."

"But—"

Hands grabbed him, dragging him back. He dug his heels into the earth, scratched and bit, tried to get his hands free, grabbing for Victor, who watched them with fathomless eyes.

"No, damn it." Why didn't Victor move? "Victor! No, don't, let me go..." More and more hands grabbed him, forced him down, pressed his head into the dirt, his world turning upside down.

Old Man Nathaniel spared him a last glance and then stepped in front of Victor. "Victor Lucien, you are accused of killing the wolf Jonathan. You are also accused of stealing a selkie skin so that you could trade it. How do you plead?"

Thoma could only see Victor's profile. He raised his head, his eyes steely, never wavering. "Not guilty."

The old man watched him. "You are accused of hunting down magical beings and killing them. How do you plead?"

"No," Thoma whispered. Fingers dug into his flesh, his cousins hissing around him.

Victor squared his shoulders.

"Don't," Thoma pleaded. "Don't…"

"Guilty."

The word rippled through the crowd forth and back, like an echo bouncing from selkie to selkie.

"The laws of the lands are one. You're found guilty of all crimes. The punishment is death by beheading."

Thoma tried a last time to fight his captors, but it was fruitless. It hurt, the mere thought of Victor being dead unbearable. Victor turned his head to him. He smiled, soft and sad. His entire posture screamed that he'd known that one day someone would come knocking, looking for him, and that he would need to pay the price.

That this was his repentance.

Thoma fought an arm free, stretching his fingers toward him. He just had to keep stretching until he could reach him.

The enormous men with the axes stepped forward.

The old man raised his hand.

The axes followed, the blades pointing to the sky. That blue, blue sky.

A sea gull cried.

A shot rang.

Everyone froze.

The shot echoed in the sudden silence. The island's magic thrummed with displeasure; Victor could feel it. It had been unhappy since he had set foot on its soil. As if it had feared something. Victor frowned and looked up. Everyone was craning their necks. His executioners put their axes down, looking toward the old man, waiting for guidance.

Victor knew where the shot had come from: the edge of the woods on the other side of the hill. Victor looked to there, and a man stepped like a ghost out of the shadows, a ghost in full combat gear.

Victor knew that silhouette.

The ghost held up an assault rifle, slowly advancing. When he reached the edge of the circle, he made a waving motion with it.

The selkies hissed but parted.

"Stephen?"

"As always to the rescue." Stephen pulled his goggles down and smiled, amused.

"What are you doing here?"

The old man shifted, his gaze switching between the two.

Stephen focused the rifle on him. "One move and there will be more than one dead body."

The old man held up his hands and stepped back. "What do you want?"

"To clean up this mess and get what is mine."

The old man nodded. "You can take him."

Stephen chuckled. "Oh, I will, but I also want the skin."

The crowd rippled, and the selkies hissed again. "It's not yours to have," they choroused, so eerie that the sound shivered down Victor's spine.

"I paid for it fair and square."

Victor kept his eyes on Stephen. There was a manic glint and greed to his expression, and he was obviously waiting for an opening.

"Who sold it to you?" The question came out of the crowd. Had the spectators gotten closer? Victor swallowed. This could go very wrong, very fast.

Stephen smiled, unmoved. "That wolf over there." His head tilted to the side, toward the groups of weres.

The selkies moved out of the way.

The weres looked uneasily around; some had narrowed their eyes at the accusation.

"Who?" Old Man Nathaniel growled, stalking in their direction. "Who dared?"

The earth shifted under their feet.

With attention shifted away from him, Thoma sat up, but he made no move to get closer to Victor again nor any attempt to rescue him.

Stephen turned slowly, his weapon still raised, and pointed a finger directly at Trevor. "This one."

"No," Trevor bristled as those around him took a cautious step away.

"Calling me a liar now?" Stephen said amused. "Victor, tell them."

All eyes went back to him. "You did bend the truth in the past, but you've never lied."

Stephen chuckled. It wasn't a nice sound. "There you have it, boy. You want to try again?"

The onlookers moved even farther away from Trevor.

"I thought we were partners?" Trevor's face turned red.

"We were," Stephen said, "but then you didn't listen. And people who don't listen are of no use to me."

"He was in the way."

Victor studied Trevor; there was a dreadful desolation in his eyes.

"He's nothing," Trevor spat.

"To you, maybe," Stephen drawled, "but not to me. I told you he was mine. I told you to keep out of it, but you didn't listen."

Victor eyed Stephen. "What are you saying?"

"It's high time for you to accept me."

"You know it doesn't work like that." Bonds were peculiar; they couldn't be forced. They needed to grow and come together on their own. And even if he wanted to bond with Stephen, Victor was already bonded to Thoma, and he'd prefer Thoma have that honor. Their bond could be broken off, a new bond made to another person, but only if Victor was willing.

He wasn't.

"It will work like that," Stephen snarled.

Victor flinched back. He'd never seen Stephen behave any way other than calm and composed. Ex-military comrades had told Victor that even when they had thrown him out, Stephen had walked with his head held high, showing no emotion about having lost the only place he'd ever felt comfortable. Now Victor saw dark and ferocious madness in his eyes. He needed to move fast and get Stephen out of here.

"Okay," Victor said, and rose slowly. He relaxed the tension in his muscles, making himself as non-threatening as he could.

"That's a good boy."

Victor pressed his teeth together and exhaled. Stephen was smiling. He almost looked like the old Stephen, the one Victor had served with—cocky and brazen. Victor should have realized when they'd met in the diner, when Stephen had looked at the waitress. He should have listened to his instincts when he'd smelled that dark undercurrent. But Victor had just been glad that at least someone from among his old comrades had remembered he still existed.

"I know where the skin is. We can get it and then we can go home."

"Yes, you and me. Finally."

Victor stepped forward, another step. Stephen's rifle sank. No one else moved, nor took any action to interfere. That was good. If everyone kept out of this, maybe Victor's plan could actually work...

"Victor." Low and broken, whispered into the wind.

The island hummed.

Stephen whirled to the side, the rifle at the ready again. His eyes found Thoma's figure in the grass; Thoma looking small and lost. "Small boy, what do you want?"

"Let Victor go."

"Why should I?"

Victor licked his lips and didn't dare to look at Thoma, hoping against hope that the selkie wouldn't say anything.

"Because he's mine."

"Then say goodbye." Stephen raised the rifle.

Victor moved and slapped the rifle upwards.

The shot went into the air; Stephen's eyes widened with his surprise.

"What are you—?" He must have read something in the lines of Victor's body, because he controlled himself. "That little whore?"

And Victor let go.

It was instinct. His parents, or had it been a teacher? Either way, someone had told him a long time ago that the wolf would always be a part of him, that it would always be there. With practice and meditation, he could contain it. But it would always be waiting, biding its time, until everything fell and Victor was swept away by it.

When hands finally dragged him backwards, Stephen's skull was caved in and his throat clawed out. His eyes were dead.

He'd never stood a chance.

THE WOOD WAS sun-warm. Victor sat on the steps leading to Maxim's office, smoking. The whole day felt like a fever dream. His hands trembled every time he thought back on it. He'd killed Stephen with his bare hands. Stephen, who had threatened his mate, yes, killed in cold blood, and Victor didn't feel any regret.

Raised voices drifted through the closed door. Maxim was interrogating Trevor. The details were pretty unsurprising. Jonathan had found out about the little operation Trevor had going on the side, hunting and killing magical beings for their most potent parts and selling them to the highest bidder. Jonathan had intended to go to the authorities and Trevor, while trying to persuade him not to, had accidentally killed him.

Trevor wouldn't live to see another day.

The selkies had returned to the sea; only the old man and the executioners remained behind.

The old man hadn't apologized, just told Victor to go.

Watching the villagers going about their day as if nothing had happened, Victor wondered if someone would come to him looking for Stephen. No, that was unlikely—more likely, someone who knew what Stephen had been doing would set themself up in the gap Stephen had left behind. Nothing would change.

Victor sighed. Let it be a problem for future-him.

"Victor."

He stamped out his cigarette and turned his head. Thoma had come close, only leaving a few paces between them. Victor tried not to make any hasty movements. Thoma had seen the monster inside him, had seen what he could do. He must be frightened.

And yet Thoma took Victor's stillness as a cue to come closer, close enough to touch. His hand was already moving toward Victor's arm.

"Don't," Victor said.

Thoma stopped, his fingers hovering over the skin, and then they made contact.

"I said—"

"—don't. I know." Thoma watched him, his face smooth and neutral. "You think I'll be repulsed."

"Yes." Victor licked his lips. "Why aren't you?"

"Because I love you."

It was a simple statement. The bond hummed between them, yet frail and brittle. If they wanted to, they could break it easily. Victor should do that, give Thoma freedom. And yet Victor felt selfish. He finally had in reach what he'd craved for so very long—somewhere to belong.

"You shouldn't," he said instead, and tried to tap out another cigarette.

Thoma settled next to him and took the cigarette away.

They watched the local weres wander around for a few minutes while the shouting at their backs quieted.

"Come with me."

Thoma shifted, then sank against his shoulder. "Not...yet. Give me time."

Not a "no," then, as Victor had anticipated. He understood. This was still Thoma's home. His family and his ancestral home were here; his very essence had seeped into this island's soil. Leaving must be unthinkable to him.

But Victor couldn't stay. He was sure that the magic he'd sensed beneath his feet meant the island was rejecting him. He'd brought chaos and death, even if it hadn't been his fault. He'd been the catalyst. With every minute, the humming under their feet grew stronger. He couldn't stay another night.

Claiming Thoma as his mate properly was all the wolf within Victor could think about, but it'd have to wait. They'd already waited a long time. What was another few weeks or months or years?

He shuddered.

"You all right?"

Victor tried a smile. It came easier than he'd expected. "Yeah, just thinking."

Someone shouted to their left—Clair came up the path, waving at them.

"The captain wants to leave and won't return for a few weeks. There's a storm coming, he says."

The island had run out of patience.

Victor rose and looked down at Thoma.

"Let me walk you down to the docks."

But Victor shook his head. "No."

Thoma furrowed his brows, ready to protest.

"The island will think I'm trying to kidnap you."

Thoma blinked and closed his eyes. The humming had turned to an aggressive buzzing.

"Oh."

Victor leaned down and kissed him deeply, drinking everything he was from him. When they parted, Thoma looked dazed.

"Write to me, Thoma."

Thoma nodded.

Victor's pack rested at his feet; he grabbed it and followed Clair down the path back to the harbor, back to the mainland.

It was high time he found a job that actually stuck, moved out of his dump of an apartment, and started rebuilding his life.

And maybe one day, Thoma would be ready to come.

Maybe soon.

Hopefully soon.

Victor turned his face into the sun and smiled.

Acknowledgments

I've always wanted to write a murder mystery. I know this story isn't one, even though there is a dead body. But Victor and Thoma clawed their way into the foreground, and the story is now more about them than the actual murder—I won't complain.

Fairytales and legends, myths and folktales have been a staple for me since I was a child. The myth of the selkies in its many incarnations holds a special place in my heart, and I hope I have done it justice. And who can say no to werewolves?

Writing a story is a beautiful thing: it's complicated, terrifying, exhausting, but when it starts to shape up under one's hands, it's the most wonderful feeling. During the creation process, there have been many people who've helped and supported me. I thank:

Duck Prints Press, especially Claire, for giving me this chance, trusting that I would have a story that readers would love to read (and buy), even if it's not quite a happy romance at the end.

My editors, who pointed out all the holes and vagueness and wonky sentences and helped me beat them into shape.

My typesetter because the interior of a book matters.

My cover illustrator, who took my vision and ran with it to create the most stunning art.

My readers, those who have supported me so far on my writer's journey, and those who picked up my work for the first time—technically this is the first book I have written beginning to end. I can't describe the feeling in my heart knowing that people have chosen to read it.

And last but not least, my spouse, who is almost prouder than me, proclaiming to everyone he meets that I write books and publish them. I love you.

About the Author:

J. D. Rivers

JD WRITES QUEER speculative fiction where they fall deeply and madly in love while figuring out the world around them. She collects hobbies as others collect books and has an unhealthy addiction to watching competitive cooking shows. JD lives close to the woods with her husband and the cutest dog in the world.

Links

Personal Website: https://jd-rivers.com/
Bluesky: https://bsky.app/profile/jd-rivers.com

Titles by J. D. Rivers

The Salt in the Sea
The Edge of a World (*Self-Published*)

Anthologies including J. D. Rivers

He Bears the Cape of Stars (author contributor)
Aim For The Heart: Queer Fanworks Inspired by Alexandre Dumas's The Three Musketeers (author contributor)

About Duck Prints Press LLC

Duck Prints Press LLC is an independent publisher based in New York State. Our founding vision is to help fanwork creators navigate the complex process of bringing their original works from first draft to print, culminating in publishing their work under our imprint. We are particularly dedicated to working with queer creators and publishing stories and artwork featuring characters from across the LGBTQIA+ spectrum.

Support Duck Prints Press on Patreon!

Find us online at our website https://duckprintspress.com/ or on social media:

Bluesky: duckprintspress
Facebook: duckprintspress
Instagram: duckprintspress
Patreon: duckprintspress
TikTok: @duckprintspress
Tumblr: duckprintspress

Goodreads: https://www.goodreads.com/user/show/129902473-duck-prints-press-llc

Storygraph: https://app.thestorygraph.com/profile/unforth

If you enjoyed this story, don't forget to leave us a review!